BLOOD IN HIS EYE . . .

Just after taking one last step and an instant before the FLNA man turned around, David Holden punched the Defender knife into the carotid artery at the right side of the man's neck. The man's eyes went wide with death as Holden averted his face so he wouldn't get blood in his own eyes or mouth, then eased the body down into the bright green foliage, almost soundlessly.

Quickly, Holden wiped the blade of the knife clean on the man's trouser leg, then sliced through web gear with it, denuding the man of weapons and equipment. Holden stole back into the trees.

The man had been armed with an Uzi. Holden took this, checking first that it seemed wholly functional. Then, donning the magazine bag, he started to move through the jungle again.

Other titles in the Defender series:

VENGEANCE

Jerry Ahern

Defender #7

A DELL BOOK

Published by
Dell Publishing
a division of
Bantam Doubleday Dell Publishing Group, Inc.
666 Fifth Avenue
New York, New York 10103

ISBN: 0-440-20331-7

Printed in the United States of America

Published simultaneously in Canada

July 1989

10 9 8 7 6 5 4 3 2 1

KRI

AUTHOR'S NOTE: The explosive / incendiary procedure used by Geoffrey Kearney in this novel is exceedingly dangerous to any person attempting it and should not be undertaken under any circumstances whatsoever.

CHAPTER

1

With the primary edge of the Defender knife, David Holden hacked at the shaft of hardwood he'd cut. When daylight came, he could build a small fire and harden the tip of the spear he'd have fabricated. After the prolonged exposure in the water, he didn't one hundred percent trust the ammunition for his Beretta and he wanted a weapon he could reach out with. Only a fool threw his knife if it were his only weapon. And the Crain Defender might be his only functioning weapon now.

Peru was the land of the anchovy (which he'd always hated on pizzas but would gladly have eaten now because he was famished), petroleum, gold, silver, cotton, sugar, tobacco (he could have used one of Rosie's cigarettes), and coffee (he might have killed for a cup given the chance). He was stuck here. Peru.

1

Maria was dead, murdered almost joyfully by Innocentio Hernandez. When the helicopter had made its pass, Maria had used her already wounded body to shield Holden from Hernandez's gunfire. Why had she done that? David Holden asked himself. It was a question he had asked himself a hundred times. He had somehow fallen into an unasked-for responsibility when Rufus Burroughs (former leader of the Patriots) had died and, unintentionally, almost unconsciously, Holden had assumed leadership of the Metro Patriots; and because of that some gave his life almost ridiculous value, either its preservation or destruction.

Innocentio Hernandez and his communist drug smugglers still lived. The roll of the innocent and the good sacrificed in the struggle—Holden's wife, Elizabeth, and their three children, Rufus Burroughs, Burroughs's wife Annette, Pete Villalobos, the enigmatically simple Maria—grew. Their deaths seemed to be an oversight of fate.

As night had fallen and he sat shivering on the riverbank, David Holden had sworn to rectify that oversight, no matter what it cost him.

He could not restore Maria, nor Elizabeth nor any of the rest to life but he could bestow upon Innocentio Hernandez a richly deserved death, the first of many more richly deserved reparations. First, Hernandez and Ortega de Vasquez, then Dimitri Borsoi. Then all of the rest of them. The first spear was cut, and Holden set it aside to begin work on the second. There would be time enough to practice with the spears. Hernandez and his men had to think that he—David Holden —was dead, and that would allow him the time he needed to hunt them.

If any among the men of Innocentio Hernandez and Hernandez's boss, Emiliano Ortega de Vasquez, stood in his way, Holden would kill if he had to. Once he had one of them down, perhaps there would be fresh ammunition for the Beretta; certainly he could claim an M-16 or an Uzi or a riot shotgun. One thing inexorably led to another and he was inured to the inevitability of death, but he would never be inured to death's aftermath like those who were the crazies of the world—the Innocentio Hernandezes or the Dimitri Borsois.

He'd laid out snares made from cut segments of green vine to catch small animals that he could eat. His stomach ached from hunger. The abdominal pain resulting from the torture he had sustained at the hands of Dimitri Borsoi before being spirited here, to the mountains of Peru, on the border with Brazil was nearly past now. And there was still another pain; perhaps killing Hernandez and the others would make that go away.

He had treaded water or swum for hours; he'd lost track of how many hours exactly. He thought about foods he'd refused to eat in the past. Like all boys Holden hadn't liked certain vegetables. He remembered all the times in his life he had rejected okra, the taste of which he'd always detested. Right now he would have eaten his broccoli, or consumed okra until he was stuffed.

His clothes were still wet and the night was cold.

It was a colder night for Maria, dead and in the ground somewhere if someone had even had the decency to bury her.

If he made it, David Holden told himself, if he killed Hernandez and Ortega de Vasquez, then he would attempt to work his way downriver into the Amazon, find a means of communicating with Tom Ashbrooke, the father of his—Holden's—dead wife, Elizabeth. Perhaps, Holden hoped, Ashbrooke could help, help to smuggle him back into the United States, to Metro.

And to Rosie Shepherd.

There was still a war to be fought in the United States. Innocentio Hernandez and Emiliano Ortega de Vasquez and men like them only fueled it, profited from it—they were not the men who fought it. With Ortega de Vasquez and his henchman Innocentio Hernandez gone, there would only be more to take their place, other men who would turn a profit on misery and death. There were always those who wished to destroy, because destruction was vastly simpler than building; and there was no shortage of destroyers from among the global terrorist network, from among the amoral street punks who would beat an old woman to death for her Social Security check, from among the self-styled idealists who saw

4

global communism as the destiny of mankind and individualism as the ultimate transgression.

The Front for the Liberation of North America. The FLNA.

As to when the war with them would stop, David Holden could not hazard a guess. Likely, not in his lifetime, because his lifetime would be short. A bullet would one day find him in the right spot at the right time and that would end it—for him. Others would go on fighting. Of that David Holden had no doubt, and through them he would live, and so would Rosie—and Rufus Burroughs.

The second spear was cut and Holden began whittling its narrowest end to a point. As with the first spear, he would fire-harden its point tomorrow. Then he'd find a village, steal a dugout canoe or a rowboat, and cross the river.

Holden's shirt was in shreds, but he would get used to the cold.

The spears finished, he sat in the dark, his arms folded across him for what warmth they could provide.

Holden still shivered.

He waited. He had all the time in the world.

CHAPTER

2

David Holden crouched before the fire, its smoke stifling in the dirt cave he had gouged. He held his breath as long as he could as he worked. He had been trained as a diver in his Navy SEAL Team days and he could hold his breath for a long time. When he could no longer hold it, he would move in a low crouch toward the cave entrance and exhale, inhale several times, again hold his breath, and reenter the cave. He could not let the smoke escape to trail upward and possibly betray his position.

In the flames, David Holden fire-hardened the points of his hardwood spears, blackening them in the frantically upward licking white-coronaed yellow.

The last of the spears was ready and he escaped the cave again, sucking air.

The arrows remained to be hardened.

He had fabricated the bow from more of the hardwood, but used greener wood so it would bend without snapping. The arrows—he had three dozen of them—were hand whittled into the proper size. Nothing but wooden points, when fire hardened they would serve against the soft flesh of men.

David Holden gulped air and reentered the cave, setting to his arrows. . . .

The Defender knife. David Holden's eyes traveled its length, assessing its features. The black synthetic handle-covering which was molded to the shape of his hand. The skull-crusher butt cap. The fighting, tsuba-like guard. With a soft stone he worked the primary edge of the Crain knife. The physical conformation of the Defender made it appear to be hollow ground, but it was flat ground instead. Holden turned the knife in his hand, putting the stone to the recurving false edge.

Somehow, he had never brought himself to sharpen the ready-to-be-sharpened spine of the blade, making the Defender a full double edge.

Was it a way of clinging to the image of civilized, law-abiding family man, college professor?

He set to sharpening the spine now. . . .

David Holden wedged his knee into the bow and notched the string. He raised the bow—it was nearly five feet in length—and drew back without an arrow in place. The draw weight was incredibly heavy to him; the muscles in his forearms, his biceps, his shoulders, were on the verge of trembling with the tension. He controlled his breathing, steadied the bow, almost mechanically letting the tension on the string ease.

Holden lifted the first of the six arrows with the poorest fire hardening. The body of a dead bird, its feathers washed clean of fleas and vermin in the river, then left to dry in the sun, had provided the fletching. He eyed the shaft beneath the bright sunlight. It was a warm spring day here. But his business was not the renewal of life, rather the taking of it.

He nocked the arrow and drew back on the bowstring as he turned toward the target he had constructed from his already torn-to-shreds shirt.

He drew the bow fully back, bringing the string nearly to his ear. He settled it. His fingers released. There was a twanging sound like some sort of giant insect buzzing his ear and the bow vibrated in his left hand as the arrow struck the mark and drove fully through the shirt into the roughly shaped bale of leaves and branches behind it. His shot was a little low at fifty yards.

David Holden smiled. . . .

Holden moved along the animal trail he had found which paralleled the road. He alternately watched for any signs of a residual force sent by Innocentio Hernandez and some handy means of crossing the river to pursue his vengeance.

He froze.

A Porta-Boat. Three men, all of them carrying weapons. He recognized one of the faces from the day he had escaped from the compound in the big Chevy Suburban with Maria—terrified—beside him. The face belonged to one of Hernandez's drug army.

He had found both of the things his eyes had searched for, watched for.

Men of Innocentio Hernandez and a boat.

Maria was dead now.

They would be dead soon.

He fell back deeper into the trees and waited. . . .

The three men moved along the river's edge, evidently sent to search for a body—his, Holden wondered?

The apparent leader, the one with the face—a ferret face with glowing black eyes—which Holden had recognized from the compound, found something of interest along the embankment and muttered something in machine-gunned Spanish too indistinct for Holden to even attempt to understand.

One of the others gestured toward where the ground rose into a jumble of rocks, like a miniature mountain, some five hundred yards to the north.

The three moved off, more rapidly than they had approached, in the direction toward which the man had gestured. Holden, watching from a distance, fixed their direction of travel clearly in his mind, then moved out of the foliage and approached the spot in the mud where they had stopped. He saw their footprints, but none of his own, and the markings of something being dragged out of the water. A boat?

Holden glanced in the direction his quarry had taken, then followed the gouged depression in the mud. The mud turned to hard earth and foliage was abundant as he penetrated deeper away from the riverbank.

Holden stopped at a mound of leaves covering a tarp. He whisked away the tarp. A lizard of some type—he had never been much for biology—scurried out of the sunlight.

He had discovered a folding Porta-Boat, so much like the one the three men had debarked from that it could have been its twin—except for the small outboard motor mounted aft.

Holden opened the gasoline cap. The tank seemed nearly full as Holden inserted a leaf snatched from the disturbed camouflage. He threw the now glistening leaf aside. He screwed the gasoline cap tightly in place. He could steal this boat—steal—and make good his river crossing, without running risk of confrontation with Innocentio Hernandez's men.

But who owned the boat? Clearly the three men had been searching whoever had used the boat, not for the boat itself, nor for his—Holden's—body as he had originally assumed. They could have tracked the boat to its hiding place just as he had. A tenderfoot Cub Scout could have found it.

Holden set down his bow, quickly re-covering the boat with the tarp, dropped to his knees, scooped back handfuls of the bright green leaves and placed them over the tarp.

He picked up his bow, turned his eyes toward the rocky mound now some six hundred yards distant and the three men disappearing over its summit. Holden broke into a run after them.

CHAPTER

3

Luther Steel rubbed sleep from his eyes, sitting up suddenly alert. His wife was in bed beside him. "Deana," Steel murmured, shaking his head. His son and daughter were asleep on the next bed. His daughter stirred, rolled over a little, and lay still.

Steel looked at his watch.

It was nearly noon.

On the motel-room chair beside the bed was the SIG-Sauer P-226 9mm pistol. Between the mattress and the box spring was the Smith & Wesson Model 66 snubby. He reached for it now, just enough of the butt of the revolver extending outward that he could get to it quickly.

He threw his feet over the side of the bed.

He stood up.

He was now a wanted man, whether officially or not, and his wife and children were marked for death just as he was. Because of his work in Metro?

Or because he could vouch for Director Cerillia that the now comatose and likely-to-die President of the United States had ordered that the Federal Bureau of Investigation construct an alliance with the Patriots in order to bring about the defeat of the Front for the Liberation of North America?

It was the latter, he knew. And Roman Makowski, de-facto President with the real President dying and the Vice President killed in the FLNA attack on the security conference, was the man behind the nearly successful attack at the safe house. If it hadn't been for Rocky Saddler being there to help in the fight which ensued—

Steel walked quickly to the window, the SIG in his right fist, the fingers of his left hand drawing back the drape and the sheer beneath it.

Rocky Saddler.

The old man sat in his car, watching them from across the parking lot. The headlights of Saddler's car blinked on and off, the agreed-upon signal that all was well.

Had Saddler gone sleepless throughout the night?

Steel closed the curtain.

He was conscious of his seminakedness. He wore nothing but his underpants as there had been no will left to unpack their meager belongings when at last they had found a motel Saddler had decreed to be safe.

Steel went into the bathroom, thought better of closing the door, set down his pistol, and urinated, sprinkling the rim of the toilet bowl a little. His aim was off. He was exhausted, despite the sleep. He snatched up a handful of toilet paper and cleaned the mess. He had a wife and daughter. Steel lowered the seat. As he moved to retrieve his gun, then go and awaken Deana, he caught sight of his face in the bathroom mirror.

And he thought of Rocky Saddler. He and Saddler were both black, but the colors of their skin were hardly the same. Steel remembered suddenly the first important assignment he'd been given in the Bureau, how conscious he'd been of his race and the need to do well, not just as well as the white guys he'd be working with, but better. He'd never wanted to believe that if one black man screwed up all black men were judged, all were diminished. So, he'd told himself "just in case" and put out the extra effort, just like he had in high school and in college and in law school. Just like he had every day before and every day since.

Saddler. Sixties at least. The medals and decorations for his wartime service, his reaction time and abilities vastly better than those of men half his age, better than Steel's own. Steel had trusted the man with the security of his family and would do so again. There was no choice and, he thought, could be no one better—maybe not even himself.

He had things to do.

First, link up with Clark Pietrowski, Bill Runningdeer, Tom LeFleur, and Randy Blumenthal.

But then what? Join the Patriots? Try somehow to confront Roman Makowski? Go to the press?

He leaned over the sink and closed his eyes.

"Lute?"

He started to swing the muzzle of the pistol toward the sound, but mind took control over reaction and he merely looked up.

She was very beautiful, always had been. She was the prettiest woman he'd ever seen and the only woman he'd ever made love to. She was wearing one of his shirts and looked pretty in it. He drew her close to him there in the bathroom doorway.

And he kissed her and her hands touched gently at his face. He leaned his head down against her shoulder and her lips brushed against his cheek. She whispered, "We'll be all right, Lute. All of us will be. I love you."

He held her so tightly he almost wept.

CHAPTER

4

The appointment with Theron Hyde wasn't for another hour. Tom Ashbrooke sat at the table farthest from the doorway of the little fish-and-chips shop, recognizing the face of the man who entered. There was no nod of recognition, the man—tall, darkly good-looking with a full shock of black hair just touched with gray, a camel-colored overcoat opening as he walked—moved quickly toward the table.

Ashbrooke stood up. "Saul, it's good to see you."

"Tom."

The two men sat.

A waitress approached, cockney struggling to emerge through her speech as she asked the newcomer to her table if he wanted to see a menu and he only ordered tea.

"It seems kind of funny, Tom."

16

"What does?" Ashbrooke smiled, lighting a cigarette from the pack beside his coffee.

"Well, I was just thinking how odd it is for an Israeli to give you a gun." The waitress approached and Saul Rothstein fell silent. As she set down the steaming cup and withdrew, Rothstein continued. "I remember the early days a lot more now than I used to. I guess I was too busy living them then." He smiled. "But there you were, this young American punk, bringing arms to us back in 1948 and only taking the money you needed to keep the operation going."

"I lied," Ashbrooke said, feeling embarrassed. "I used some of the money for food and cigarettes too."

Rothstein lit a cigarette. "Yes. Well, I'd assumed as much. Naturally, when you called, well—you could have asked for a bloody tank and I'd have gotten it for you."

"A pistol'll do fine. Just for insurance." Ashbrooke grinned.

"In the pocket of my coat, of course. When I get up to leave, I'll leave the coat behind—"

"—and I go running after you," Ashbrooke picked up, "palming the gun before I give you back the coat."

"Palm the spare magazines, too, you'd better," Rothstein nodded, sipping at his tea. "This is awful."

"I figured the coffee'd be safer this time of day."

"Was it?" Rothstein smiled.

"No."

"How's Diane?"

Ashbrooke leaned stubbed out his cigarette. "She's fine. Beautiful as ever."

"I'd naturally assumed that," Rothstein said, looking down at his tea. "Send her my best, would you?"

"Always."

"Not enough you came out of one of the dirtiest businesses in the world smelling like the proverbial rose, but you wound up with the most beautiful woman since Helen of Troy." And Rothstein laughed. "I was always glad—well—that it, ahh, never came between us."

"So was I," Ashbrooke told him.

"Why does a respectable, retired businessman need a gun in London—or is it—" And Rothstein stopped in midsentence. "Look, Tom, if you've found some of the men responsible for the deaths of your daughter and your grandchildren, I have some people who can—"

"No. But maybe one day I will. I was just sitting back. I told myself I was too old for this shit. Then this girl called me. Her name's Rose. Sounds more like the kind of girl you'd call Rosie, maybe. A nice girl. Ex-cop. She and David, ahh—Anyway, David's been kidnapped. By the FLNA. He's a big leader in—"

"The Patriots. I read the newsmagazines too. So you're here to talk with Theron Hyde. Lucky I

18

brought you the spare magazines. Set it up through Hilly?"

"I didn't want to get your people involved."

"Mossad's already involved. One of the favorite FLNA targets is synagogues. Ever since your American President was struck down and the Vice President killed—we lost an observer at the security conference, Moishe Ben Israel."

"My God, Boris?"

Rothstein laughed. "He hated it when you called him by his real name."

"That was the Russian in him, I always said. Change your government, change your name."

"Rothstein laughed a little hollowly, looking at his hands again. "I understand he died instantly during the first explosion. Hyde is a very dangerous man," Rothstein continued, looking up. "But you already know that. The Brits—like your friend Hilly in SIS—won't back you up like we could. It's not their fault, but they hate doing anything dirty on their own ground. Whereas"—Rothstein smiled—"I'm only a diplomat."

"And I'm Santa Claus."

"Hmm. Can we back you up? What you find out might be useful to us too."

Ashbrooke considered Rothstein's argument. Hyde would have heavy security, reportedly always did. The meeting was to be for five minutes, and was done as a courtesy only. That was why Ashbrooke wanted the gun. Hyde would likely tell him nothing without being coaxed a bit. "What are you suggesting?"

"Anything you think would help. The worst that can happen to me is they'll send me back to Israel. I've got a lovely niece—her husband died on the Strip not too long ago—who's dying to feed me dinner every night and a pension and an ever-growing number of rich American female tourists who'd love asking me how I got my battle scars. It's that whole Paul Newman image from the cinema, you know. Heroic Israeli freedom fighter. I even have the blue eyes." Rothstein grinned.

"All right. Then we go all the way and put the bag on Hyde and keep him until he tells me how to find David. After that, flush him down the toilet for all I care."

Rothstein laughed. "I thought you'd really retired, Tom."

CHAPTER

5

David Holden stalked the stalkers. For clearly
that was what the men of Innocentio Hernandez
had been doing. There was a small house a mile or
so above and beyond a village set in a shallow,
dish-shaped valley. The house seemed precariously balanced on the side of a promontory of rock
almost devoid of vegetation.

The three men, assault rifles in patrolling positions, had moved into a ragged semicircle as
they'd closed with the house. Why was clear. To
eliminate an enemy. Any enemy of Innocentio
Hernandez was not automatically a friend to
David Holden, but certainly a potential ally.

He shivered as a cool breeze dried sweat across
his back.

The men were clearly going to attack the house.
Who lived there?

David Holden fingered the string of his bow.

One of the three men—the one he had recognized—had been using a radio periodically as they'd moved into position, clearly summoning someone else or reporting to Hernandez, perhaps both.

Who was in this house perched on the side of a giant rockpile?

David Holden waited. . . .

Rose Shepherd checked her watch. The Timex Ironman was a little mannish-looking, but she'd stake its toughness against David's Rolex diving watch. And this wasn't exactly a social function for which she was waiting. She was crouched in the autumn scrub brush a hundred yards back from the road, her M-16 beside her. She was not wearing her black BDUs, because they would merely call attention to her, but because of the chill on the air today she was wearing a heavy woollen sweater over the cotton blouse. She wiped the palms of her hands down along her blue-jeaned thighs.

Where was Clark Pietrowski?

If the car was coming, it should be there on the road at the base of the rise in the next few minutes. If it didn't come, was Clark in trouble? She couldn't take the collaboration with the FBI falling apart now. With David—

"Shit," she hissed through her teeth. This Thomas Ashbrooke, the father of David's dead wife. Could he really do anything? Or was he just

an old warhorse who didn't know when to quit?
Although he hadn't struck her that way.

And then the call had come from London to
Mitch Diamond, the message for her that a package would be dropped off for her and she shouldn't
worry what to do with it, just not lose it. The contents of the package, at first glance, had seemed to
be an ordinary attaché case. When she opened the
case however she found a peculiar telephone inside. Mitch Diamond had looked at it, then pro-
nounced it "a scrambler/descrambler—that's
what they call it. You stick the telephone receiver
you dialed from into the notch there and the call
goes through the unit inside the case and you
speak through the other handset. The person
you're talkin' to has a unit just like it, either porta-
ble like this or desk mounted. Doesn't matter.
Your voice goes to them scrambled and they
descramble. Their voice comes to you scrambled
and you descramble. Pretty simple. Now, with
most of these, if whoever's listening has a descrambler or records the conversation and runs it
through a descrambler, they've got you. But a ca-
sual operator-observed call or something like that,
you're secure. Now, this one"—And Mitch Diamond pointed to what looked like a small computer keyboard in one corner of the unit—"with
this one, looks like you can key the machines to
specific settings, which means that no direct moni-
toring would be possible because the settings
would be wrong and it'd take somebody a while to

unravel the code setting and then descramble.
Maybe it's more sophisticated than that. I could
take it apart and—" But she'd stopped him at that.
Because it was clear that Tom Ashbrooke intended
to use the device and a similar one on his own end
of the conversation so they could be in direct contact, possibly with the code he'd given her or without it. She didn't know. She'd never been to spy
school and they hadn't covered stuff like this at the
police academy.

A car came along the road. She didn't recognize
it but Clark Pietrowski would have been a fool to
drive a recognizable car anyway.

Rose Shepherd brought the M-16 to her shoulder and waited. . . .

More men had come up from the village, one of
them speaking briefly with the apparent leader of
the trio of Hernandez's men Holden had first spotted at the river. More of Hernandez's men? Or
simply local toughs they'd bought for the occa-
sion? Holden didn't know. He didn't care but he
was grateful he had not gone into the village seek-
ing aid.

Ten men took up positions around the house.
One of the Hernandez men was using the radio
handset. Some of the newcomers carried radios as
well, in addition to their rifles and shotguns and
machetes.

David Holden started to move. . . .

* * *

The car stopped and Clark Pietrowski stepped out from behind the wheel. "Rosie?"

"Up here!" It was dumb to shout to him, she realized as she did it. What if somebody was in the back of the car? Not that she distrusted Clark. The past-retirement-age FBI agent was a good cop and a good man, and not particularly in that order. But somebody could have sandbagged him in the car or something. The damage—if there were any— was done. She stood up, slowly, the M-16 locked beside her right hip. "You alone?"

"Yeah. I can see you aren't." He laughed back, gesturing with his empty hands as if he were spraying out an assault rifle or a submachine gun.

She smiled, lowering the weapon just a little, starting down from the rise. Clark was walking toward her, talking in a loud voice, gradually lowering it as they neared each other. "I heard from Luther, like I told you. And I checked with Runningdeer, LeFleur, and Blumenthal. Luther was the only one they tried making a hit on yet, but maybe that's because the rest of us pulled a vanishing act on them. You may be getting some new recruits, Rosie."

She laughed, coming to a halt about two yards from him, the muzzle of her rifle pointed to the ground. "Yeah, well, I don't know, Clark. We usually don't take guys as young as you."

Pietrowski grinned. "Seriously, kid, we got big troubles. I figured you should know what we

know. And I got a message for you from Mr. Cerillia. Seems like he did a little digging for you after
all. David was alive—"

"Was!" She was directly in front of him in two
strides, her heart in her mouth. She'd always
heard the expression and for the first time in her
life she knew how it felt.

"Easy, kid. No reason to think he still isn't—
alive, I mean. If they'd wanted him dead it would
have been a whole hell of a lot simpler to kill him
Stateside rather than ship him out of the country.
Cerillia learned about it from some folks in DEA
who owed him a favor. David was with a guy by
the name of Innocentio Hernandez. The Feds
would have tried to stop it, but they didn't get the
information until it was too late. Standard infor-
mant shit. So—"

"You're beautiful," she told him, throwing her
arms around his neck and almost bashing him in
the head with her M-16. . . .

David Holden nocked an arrow. One of the men
who'd come up from the village was about sixty-
five yards away, his back to David. But the terrain
was too open for too long behind him to come up
on him safely with a knife. Resting beside the man
—he observed the house through binoculars—was
an M-16. On the man's waist was a pistol which
Holden hoped would either prove serviceable or
be a 9mm with serviceable ammunition he could
use in his liberated Beretta 92F.

Holden's right thumb master joint lay beside his cheek. He swung the arrow on line as the man started to move and let fly. The vibration of the bow sent a chill through his body. The arrow flew true, the man's body taking the hit at the small of his back. He rocked forward, but Holden knew he was still alive.

Holden was up and running. Shifting the bow to his left hand, he grabbed one of the spears from the improvised sling he'd fabricated for them out of one of his shirtsleeves and some of the fishing line from the hollow handle of his knife. As he charged toward the man, the man rolled onto his back, eyes wide with pain, but his hand reaching for the pistol at his hip. It was a revolver, and even if the man didn't shoot him, a stray shot would alert the others that something was wrong.

Holden hurtled the spear with his full body-weight behind it. The spear impacted the man high, through the thorax. His eyes widened more, then his expression became blank as he crumpled to the rocks.

Holden was on him the same instant, ripping the spear from the man's throat, ready to drive it home again. There was no need.

Quickly, Holden searched him, snatching off the pistol belt and the half-opened flap holster with the revolver partially drawn. A ditty bag. A cheap switchblade. Cigarettes, but bloodstained. A disposable lighter. He threw away the cigarettes, grabbed up the rest along with the M-16 and the binoculars, then ran into the trees.

Holden kept running, only sagging to his knees in a strange mixture of exhaustion and relief once he was nearly a hundred yards into the trees.

The rifle. He inspected it quickly. It was chamber loaded and took military ball. There were three twenty-round magazines and one thirty up the magazine well. Clearing the weapon, he broke it open, pulling the bolt, checking the bore for obvious signs of corruption. The rifle was lightly oiled and appeared well maintained. He replaced the bolt, locking the action to the barrel assembly again. He loaded one of the twenties up the well, worked the charging handle, and set the safety. The twenties were less likely to stack and set than a thirty.

The revolver was a Taurus in .357 Magnum, approximately the same size and configuration as a K-Frame Smith & Wesson. He checked the cylinder. The blued six-gun was chambered with .38 Special Plus P's, hollowpoints of European manufacture. Holden cinched the belt around his waist.

He searched the ditty bag and found an unopened package of Camels. He rectified that immediately, not daring to light one here, but sniffing at the freshly opened pack, almost tasting the smoke. Next, he discovered a Hershey bar, unopened, the wrapper looking relatively new. He opened the wrapper, inspected the candy bar carefully, then devoured half of it, holding his stomach.

Carefully he replaced cigarettes and candy in the ditty bag, along with the magazines for the M-16 he'd taken from the pistol belt. Holden grabbed up his bow and his bloodied spear and ran.

CHAPTER

6

The pistol Rothstein had brought him was almost stereotypically Israeli, a Walther PPK in .22 Long Rifle, the barrel from a Walther PP and protruding well past the front of the slide, threaded on the outside for a silencer. Despite its being the favorite of Israeli assassins and executive protection personnel, Thomas Ashbrooke had never been a great fan of .22's of any variety for serious antipersonnel use. But he understood the Israeli motivation. In a crowd, regardless of the intended use, there was less chance of overpenetration, less chance of ricochets, and .22's were easier to use effectively with a silencer of reasonable length and girth.

He fisted the pistol in his pocket as he sat in the backseat of the Jaguar sedan.

The glass was darkly tinted, but Thomas Ashbrooke could see through it clearly enough. What unfolded continually before him was not dissimilar to some sort of London tourism video showing a cross section of young and old, teenagers with bizarre clothing and even more bizarre hairstyles, businessmen in dark topcoats, even the occasional bowler hat. Umbrellas were carried by the cautious or the traditional. The sky was clear for London this time of the year, the purple of the sunset visible in bits and snatches between rooftops.

The door of the Mercy Club, a private club for card-playing foreign nationals of which Theron Hyde was not a member, but the owner, opened. A crew-cut man in an overly well-tailored tweed jacket stepped through and onto the steps, looking up and down the street.

Ashbrooke glanced at his watch.

Time.

He worked the Jaguar's door handle and stepped out onto the curb, his ears instantly assailed by the sounds of traffic. The tweed-jacketed man looked in his direction knowingly and Ashbrooke nodded. Ashbrooke leaned into the car, saying loudly enough to be heard by his friend Saul Rothstein, "Phillip. I won't be needing you for fifteen minutes. Get some coffee if you like. Never mind the door." He slammed the sedan's left-side passenger door and walked toward the steps where the tweed-jacketed man stood staring at him. "I take it you're in the employ of Mr. Hyde?" He refrained from even thinking about Dr. Jekyll.

"Mr. Ashbrooke?"

"Yes."

"Mr. Hyde didn't mention you lived in London."

"Ohh—Phillip, you mean. Chauffeurs around an old friend. Sort of on loan. You're American."

"Was. Come inside, please."

The doorman had the door opening as they reached it. The bodyguard or aide or whatever he was let Ashbrooke pass inside ahead of him, to look for obvious weapons. There was a dinging sound as Ashbrooke passed through the doorway and into the carpeted foyer. A metals detector, Ashbrooke presumed.

"Your keys, maybe?" His hand was under his coat, either to reach for something innocuous or for a shoulder-holstered handgun.

Ashbrooke looked at him and smiled. "My gun. Would you like to keep it for me?"

"Just put it on the table there, please"—and with his head, his hand still under his coat, he gestured toward a small table with a very small lamp on it near the entrance.

Slowly, Ashbrooke removed the 1934 Beretta .380 from under his jacket. He set it on the table. The Beretta, borrowed from Rothstein's glove compartment, was a wholly functional, wholly untraceable drop gun. The .22 caliber PPK was still in his coat pocket. "Want me to pass through again?" And Ashbrooke started walking toward the doorway.

The tweed-jacketed man drew his right hand

from beneath his coat, a cigarette in his fingers. As he lit it with a Colibri lighter, he said through an exhalation of smoke, "No—I guess not."

"Happy to, if you'd like."

Tweed-jacket shook his head and started down along the low stairs just beyond the foyer. Ashbrooke shrugged his shoulders and fell in after him. This was too easy, he thought, but sometimes the obvious was like that.

The clock on the wall was an elaborate and very large grandfather that looked to be of mixed parentage by a cuckoo clock. Ashbrooke noted the time. If it was correct, Saul Rothstein and his Mossad boys would be through the front and back doors in about four minutes.

They crossed an attractively appointed lounge area with easy chairs arranged neatly but haphazardly, a fireplace dominating the far wall and small reading lamps and tables near to each chair.

"Off night for the club?"

"Usually is kind of quiet until later on. Maybe Mr. Hyde will ask if you'd like to join. As a non-Brit you'd be eligible."

"How about my bank account?"

"You have to discuss that with Mr. Hyde himself."

Ashbrooke merely nodded.

They moved up more low stairs and into a wide, similarly appointed corridor—paneling, subdued lighting, soft carpeting—and along its length in relative silence. Perhaps there was another metal detection system somewhere along the corridor, or perhaps Hilly—God, would Hilly and the old boys be pissed that the Israelis were going to bag Hyde—perhaps Hilly was so trusted that Hyde's guard was down.

If that were the case, Hyde was not only evil, he was stupid.

They arrived at a doorway and tweed-jacket shifted a wall-mounted light fixture left and beneath the light's backing was a lock with a key slot. The self-proclaimed former American inserted a key and the wooden door, like two others Ashbrooke had passed, opened on a buzzer, popping outward at the jam. The man opened the door fully to reveal a metal door behind it. At the side of the door was another key slot. Another key was inserted and the door opened. A subtly luxurious but apparently largely stainless steel private elevator car was revealed.

"Down or up?" Ashbrooke asked.

"Sideways." Tweed-jacket smiled. He ushered Ashbrooke inside and the door immediately thwacked shut with a pneumatic slap and hiss, tweed-jacket remaining on the other side.

Motion. And, indeed, it was sideways, right to left. The elevator car stopped, then rotated (slowly) a full 180 degrees, as best Thomas Ashbrooke could judge.

The door didn't open.

A voice, very British but somehow a little effeminate, came over the speaker mounted beside the panic phone. "Mr. Ashbrooke, my electronic sensors tell me you are carrying. A drawer will open. Please place your weapon inside."

A panel near the panic phone opened and Tom Ashbrooke took the little .22 caliber PPK from his coat pocket, then deposited it into the drawer.

"The spare magazines may remain with you. The gun will be returned when you leave."

"Thanks. I did ask your big friend out there if he wanted me to pass through your security system again, you know."

"I'd advise no chest X-rays for at least a year. You've just had the equivalent of six." There was no trace of sarcasm in the disembodied and slightly annoying voice, no trace at all.

"Marvelous. I've always wanted to have the glow of good health about me," Ashbrooke told the wall speaker.

There was the sound of suppressed laughter and the door opened. Ashbrooke saw a man sitting at the very far side of a long, rather narrow office. But, unlike the decor of the club floor through which Ashbrooke had moved in company with the man in the tweed jacket, it was more feminine than masculine in decor. There were even curtains, which were drawn back. They would let in sunshine at the right hour, Ashbrooke supposed, but the view through the window was so distorted as to make it obvious that, rather than glass, there were several thicknesses of Plexiglas between the room and the outside world.

A man—rather slight of build—stood up from behind the immaculate desk. "I'm Theron Hyde, Mr. Ashbrooke." Hyde wore a suit of gray, the gray so oddly shaded—or perhaps it was only the light—there was almost a light rose cast to it.

Ashbrooke stepped out of the elevator, walking slowly toward the desk. As Ashbrooke neared the desk, he realized it wasn't the light playing tricks, but the suit was actually a soft rose-tinged gray color. "A pleasure to meet you. Forgive the gun, but as we hadn't met I had no idea of what to expect."

"Israeli, isn't it?"

"It's a German Walther."

"I meant the treatment, not the maker."

"Got me. I know they use Walther .22's sometimes, but this one I got from an old pal in the arms business." That wasn't wholly a lie.

He was judging the time. Two minutes to go until Saul Rothstein's men would attempt the penetration. As Ashbrooke walked closer to the desk, he glanced back toward the walls on both sides of the elevator. There was no evidence of where his gun might have been deposited.

"I don't wish to sound rude, Mr. Ashbrooke," Theron Hyde said, walking around to the side of his desk, "but, like your own, my time is valuable. How may I help you, exactly? And please, sit down."

Ashbrooke angled toward the chair to which Hyde's limp-wristed hand gestured. But he didn't sit. "I understand you are heavily involved in brokering drugs around the world as an assist to general financing of terrorist activities and the acquisition of arms."

Hyde's eyes, for all the prissy manner, didn't even blink.

Ashbrooke sat down. "My son-in-law, David Holden, one of the leaders of the Patriots in the United States, has been kidnapped by forces allied to the Front for the Liberation of North America and I believe you can tell me who is supplying the drugs which are moved into North America and sold on the streets there in order to finance FLNA activities. Can you?"

Hyde perched on the near corner of his leather-topped desk. "You ask very frank questions, Mr. Ashbrooke. And I am sorry, truly, for the apparent plight of your son—or son-in-law, rather—but you are grievously misinformed."

"I am not misinformed, sir. But am I to take it from that that you will not help me?"

"I cannot."

"Will not," Ashbrooke corrected.

Hyde's little body visibly tensed and his left hand, which had been toying with the edge of an elaborate pen-and-pencil stand, drifted toward its center.

An alarm button, perhaps. Ashbrooke spoke quickly, not standing, keeping his hands still. "I wish you'd reconsider, Mr. Hyde." About thirty seconds as he judged it on his mental clock, then

37

Saul Rothstein's men would be starting in. "But if you won't—all I want is another name to go to— then I'll have to try elsewhere." Now he stood slowly, Hyde's hand no longer moving. "Thank you very much for your time."

Hyde smiled. "I'm pleased to see that you're a reasonable, fellow, Mr. Ashbrooke. Good day."

"Good evening is perhaps more appropriate," Ashbrooke smiled, glancing at his watch. *Bingo,* he almost said.

"Good evening, indeed."

Ashbrooke saw no hand offered, didn't offer his. He turned and started back for the elevator. Where were Rothstein's men?

And then he heard movement behind him. Theron Hyde was screaming.

Ashbrooke wheeled. Hyde's right hand was no longer limp, but rigid, smashing down at the center of the pen-and-pencil holder—apparently activating a silent alarm, because Ashbrooke heard no buzzing, no bells. At the window were distorted images of men, their faces covered. A spray of liquid came from something which looked like a fire extinguisher and the room suddenly filled with a smell that was all too familiar: gasoline.

A grenade was lobbed through a hole which seemed to be growing at the center of the Plexiglas shielding. The gasoline was eating through. Ashbrooke threw his hands over his ears and turned his face away, scrunching his eyes tight shut against the brilliant flash, which was almost blinding even as he perceived it through his lids. His ears were ringing slightly.

He realized he'd fallen to his knees.

As Ashbrooke stood up, Rothstein's men were punching through the hole in the Plexiglas. Theron Hyde writhed on the floor, screaming. One of Rothstein's men shouted something. Ashbrooke couldn't quite hear the words. As the man's right hand brandished a Walther PPK with an eight-inch silencer at the muzzle, Ashbrooke gambled and dropped flat.

There was a sound, had to be, but Ashbrooke didn't hear it.

Ashbrooke rolled onto his back and looked toward the elevator door.

Tweed-jacket. There was a pistol in the man's left hand and a small submachine gun—a Mini-Uzi —in his right. But his knees were buckling and he fell back against the elevator door as the opening closed and his body caught there, unmoving.

Ashbrooke got to his feet.

The same Israeli who'd shot tweed-jacket handed him a pistol, silencer and all.

Ashbrooke took it, working up the slide-mounted thumb safety, his finger going into the trigger guard. The man gestured to keep an eye on the elevator.

Ashbrooke did.

Then, seconds later, he heard the dull roar of a

human voice again. "Come on, sir! We're moving now!"

Ashbrooke turned from the elevator, ran for the hole in the window, past two of the Israelis, their submachine guns at the ready, were flanking the window on either side.

Quickly he was into the evening air and away from the nauseating smell of gasoline.

"Petrol," one of the Israelis said. "Best thing yet for Plexiglas."

Ashbrooke nodded, shoving the suppressed Walther .22 under his coat.

A van. Hyde was already disappeared inside.

Ashbrooke started to climb in and was dragged back. A Mercedes. Ashbrooke ran toward it; the one Israeli who'd given him the pistol and the two who'd guarded the withdrawal were racing toward it with him. Ashbrooke half fell into the backseat, one of the men with the Uzis jumped in with him, then the one who'd given him the pistol. The second man with an Uzi was into the front seat as the Mercedes sped away from the curb before the passenger doors were closed.

The van was disappearing around the corner at the end of the block.

Thomas Ashbrooke fingered his pistol, working the safety down and on.

"I'm not as young as I used to be, Saul," he said to his friend, driving the Mercedes.

"Nor are any of us, Tom. But think about how exciting it'll all seem when you tell Diane about it, hmm?" And Saul Rothstein laughed, then so did Tom Ashbrooke. It really had been exciting. But somehow he felt the excitement was just starting. And the charm of it might pale easily.

CHAPTER

7

The nine remaining men were settled into their positions, although it was unclear to David Holden just what their intent might be. From the deployment, they could have been preparing to assault the house, or merely to saturate it with gunfire.

Strapped around his waist was the Taurus .357 Magnum, the .38 Special Plus P's loaded. On his back was the M-16 with one of the twenty-round magazines up the well, the other two twenties and the thirty in the ditty bag. He could practically taste the opened package of Camels in the bag, but circumstances had not allowed him to light one yet.

He tightened the sling of the M-16.

Holden picked up his bow.

He nocked an arrow.

Nine men remained.

He drew back on the bow.

Holden settled on the spinal chord of the man crouched near a bracken of scrub brush and bright, broad-leafed low foliage. There were rocks just beyond.

The man shifted his position slightly.

Holden had determined that his bow shot true for lateral adjustment, but elevation was hard to determine precisely. It was for that reason he held on the spinal cord. A hit anywhere along its length would do the job.

Holden let the arrow fly.

The man's body went rigid for a second.

Then it flopped forward.

The arms vibrated, pulsed, but only in muscle spasms.

Now there were only eight men.

David Holden looked from side to side as he ran forward, his spear at the ready. But it was not needed.

Quickly, Holden took the M-16 from the dead body. A GI-style pistol belt—it bore a label reading that it was made in Taiwan—was at the dead man's waist. A black leather flap holster worn crossdraw. Holden opened it. The handgun inside was an automatic pistol, a Star in 9mm, one of the large-capacity variety of recent vintage. An excellent pistol—one of the men in camp carried one back home. "Home," Holden whispered. A rough camp and a collection of sheds and tents. A sun-warmed shower, warmed-over meals after a raid. Rosie. He closed his eyes for an instant. The Star was an excellent pistol. This one, however, was ill maintained and looked as if it might have been run over by a truck. But the ammo in it—Holden checked the magazine pouches on the belt—all of the ammo looked pristine.

He took the man's M-16, the pistol belt, the knapsack, more ammo for the handgun, and a few magazines for the M-16. Unfortunately, the magazines and the M-16 were in as bad shape as the abused handgun. He gathered a Swiss Army knife cheapie copy and another candy bar. It was a Snickers bar and seemed fresh. Although he normally didn't like nuts, his stomach still rumbled with hunger. So he took it also.

The dead man bore no identification on his body.

David Holden gathered up his new possessions, withdrawing quietly to cover in the trees.

He ate half the candy bar. He loaded the fresh 9mm Parabellum rounds into the magazines for his liberated Beretta. The ammo was a European brand he recognized; albeit the bullet construction was full metal case, it would do nicely. He stripped the .223 from the badly treated M-16 magazines. They might have proven useful—with time, solvent and oil or some Break-Free CLP, and a range to test the magazines after ministering to them. Now, he buried them in a shallow grave he dug with the pocket knife. He threw the knife into the little hole and kicked the dirt over it.

Time was meaningless. If the Hernandez men

started their attack on the house, it might prove all the easier to kill them while their attention was otherwise engaged.

The second M-16 was in terrible condition. He stripped out the bolt, dismantled the pistol the dead man had carried, and threw the M-16 and the frame of the pistol into the brush near him.

The bow might still prove useful.

He picked it up.

David Holden moved on, about a hundred yards from where he'd dumped the rifle and the frame of the pistol, and deposited the pistol's slide and the M-16's bolt in the thorny shrubbery.

A cardinal rule in survival was never to leave anything behind you which could be turned against you.

He kept moving.

He would try to whittle the odds down. Eight now.

Holden took another bite of his candy bar.

He looked for another target.

CHAPTER

8

At the Wisconsin border with Illinois there was a joint state police roadblock, the Wisconsin troopers blocking southbound traffic while their Illinois counterparts blocked traffic moving north. Each car was inspected, each occupant's papers checked.

The whole situation reminded Geoffrey Kearney of Eastern Europe, except the police were generally more polite and the papers were merely driver's license, registration, and insurance. But the police weren't hoping to catch illegal motor vehicle operators; they were still looking, Kearney knew, for the supposed Patriot killers who had claimed the lives of those at the farm where he had first rendezvoused after infiltrating across the U.S.-Canadian border.

Harriet.

Her father had been murdered by the Front for

the Liberation of North America, her estranged husband was part of the FLNA group which had attacked a school bus, and it was the FLNA who had come to her farm to kill her. Harriet had died. Kearney had been unable to prevent her death even though he had seen to it, with Harriet's help, that none of the FLNA personnel had left the farm alive.

The press—giving some official line? Kearney wondered—was sticking to the story that "a group of gunmen, suspected members of the outlawed vigilante group calling itself 'the Patriots,' " had been responsible for the killings.

Kearney was less than impressed with the shallow details. At least, he reflected, smiling as he listened to another news bulletin over the car radio, Eastern Bloc nations got their propaganda better.

The roadblock safely behind him, none of his weapons discovered in the specially modified Ford LTD with its police interceptor engine, Kearney glanced at his maps as he drove on the more or less deserted highway. A business card from a Milwaukee tavern had been found on the body of one of the FLNA dead. But the tavern had been closed, out of business, when Kearney reached it. By discreetly canvassing the neighborhood he'd learned the owner of the tavern had a brother in Chicago who owned a restaurant. A quick call to the SIS man who was head of the Midwestern United States station pinned down the restaurant and the name of the brother. It was the most solid lead he had and, because of the lead, he was diverting to Chicago now. The original plan had been to make all good speed through Wisconsin, across Illinois, and South toward Metro, to assess the current situation there. If the best opportunity for tracking down the Russian, Borsoi, had seemed likely to be found in developing leads along the Atlantic coast near Cedar Ridge Islands, where Borsoi had plummeted into the ocean during a fight aboard a helicopter with this David Holden fellow, he had planned to go East. But now Chicago was his destination.

His mission, as his superiors in British Secret Intelligence had put it obliquely but succinctly, was to find Borsoi and kill him. He was to determine if Borsoi was the boss of the FLNA and, if not, find that fellow and kill him. Ostensibly, all as a favor to Canada. But Kearney realized the real implications. With the FLNA running rampant over the United States and the installation of the ultraliberal Roman Makowski as de facto President of the United States, Great Britain herself was in danger.

Economic destabilization in the West's most powerful nation was already being more than subtly felt in world money markets. The pound, so historically linked to the health of the dollar, was sliding steadily and rapidly. There was chaos in the money markets of Japan. Global financial collapse was ever becoming a more real possibility, and with economic destabilization, political and social upheaval were inevitable.

Already in the Carribean, an area where many investors who were British subjects were heavily invested, there was sporadic violence. The Arab oil cartel spoke openly of substantial price increases because of reduced oil consumption in America. Factories no longer could get personnel to work at night, as the danger of random violence was too great. Some factories were closed. Travel was confined to only what was necessary, by and large, and the hapless traveler might easily find himself inadvertently stumbling into an FLNA raid or a battle between the FLNA and the Patriots or the police or military.

Kearney smiled. The situation reminded him of the old W. C. Fields rejoinder, "I went to Philadelphia and it was closed." The United States was becoming a massive Philadelphia in the Fieldsian sense.

Exactly what good might result from the assassination of the FLNA leader in America was not all that clear. Certainly, a time of disorganization and disorientation, but couldn't the fellow just as well be replaced and FLNA activities go right on? And Roman Makowski's political bents didn't suggest that a heroic and well-planned government intervention would cut the FLNA to the quick amid the ensuing chaos or capitalize on the situation even in the slightest.

Makowski seemed bent on negotiating with the

FLNA, bent on enforcing the idea that the FLNA war was essentially over and now was a time of healing.

Makowski was an ass, Kearney thought.

And he didn't think he was alone in holding that opinion.

What did seem clear was that the United States, like England, itself a model of political stability for all the world, was on the edge of an abyss of violence. Civil war or revolution, perhaps the two, would soon be unstoppable and Roman Makowski was more a catalyst in the brew than anything the FLNA had done.

Years before, Kearney had thought of retiring to New Mexico someday, having fallen in love with the American Southwest.

He smiled, saying under his breath, "Unrequited love." He lit a cigarette.

The name of the fellow who owned the restaurant was Roy Dumbrowski; his brother Dan was the disappeared Milwaukee tavern owner. Kearney placed the location on a Chicago street map.

He turned onto something called the Edens Expressway, which looked like the most direct route to the restaurant.

He had visited Chicago before. A well-organized city, it usually ran like a well-oiled machine. And the police—the head of station who had gotten him the name of the restaurant had started to warn him that Chicago police were tough.

Kearney knew that already, and considered

Chicago PD one of the truly top-drawer major-city police units in the world.

But he wasn't looking forward to meeting with them professionally just now.

CHAPTER

9

Number eight died hard; two of Holden's arrows were necessary to bring him down and then a quick swipe across the neck with the Defender knife's primary edge silenced him.

As a boy, while part of a school field trip group, he had seen a woman's purse stolen on the street after she'd been knocked carelessly to the sidewalk. Out of all the men on that street in front of the museum, not one had raced to her aid until the purse snatcher was well gone, nor had anyone tried to pursue the man or stop him. For the rest of that day and, at times, for years after that, David Holden had remembered the look of fear and pain on the woman's face, been able to visualize her run stockings and skinned knees and the tears which had flowed from her eyes as she'd sat there on the sidewalk trying to cover her bloodied knees with her skirt.

It did not escape David Holden that he was taking human life now, or that human life—even that of men who were drug dealers or killers—was unique, irreplaceable, and sacred. But he had made a choice early in his life that there was a decided and important difference between right and wrong. And to stand idly by while wrong was being perpetrated was in itself a wrong. He could not stand idly by. Whoever was in the house might be more evil than these men, perhaps. But what was he to do? These men might be in his way as he went to dispense his personal justice to Innocentio Hernandez and Emiliano Ortega de Vasquez. But, all of that aside, while they lived they would keep on doing what they were doing, profiting from the misery of others by the sale of drugs, promoting warfare for their own personal profit, and feeding off death.

Not this one. Not anymore.

The man had to have weighed over three hundred pounds and smelled badly of body odor and fecal material. Holden robbed him of ammunition only, leaving the weapons—ill cared for—and the magazines for them hidden (the weapons he partially dismantled) in the tree cover. The man's head had been crawling with lice and Holden, although he knew he hadn't been close enough to the fellow to pick up on the infestation, felt crawly anyhow.

With enough .223, both loose and magazined for a substantial gun battle, and more 9mm Parabellum for his pistol, Holden moved on toward man number seven.

Holden doubted there would be time to knock him out. Either a radio transmission would uncover the fate of the three dead men or the attack would begin.

As David Holden returned to the edge of the tree line, the latter of his suspicions was confirmed.

Automatic weapons fire broke out from the seven who remained in the ragged circle surrounding the house. The two windows at the front of the house were shattered immediately, the chimney cap shot off, and chunks of the roof's overhanging eaves were blasted away.

And then the gunfire ceased. And from the direction of the three original Hernandez men, a voice shouted, barely audible from Holden's position, and barely intelligible because of the poor quality of the English.

"We have you there inside *la casa*. Drop out your weapons and surrender up or be died!"

"Hmm," Holden murmured. The fellow had a natural flare for language. Whoever was in the house, who had so unskillfully left behind the boat, was wanted alive. "Hmm," Holden murmured again. Possibilities.

The seven men began advancing on the house, closing the ring, covering their tightening skirmish line with misdirected assault-rifle fire.

There was answering fire from the house—from

a shotgun, by the sound of it. The answering fire had no visible effect on the attackers. Not surprising. It took great skill to be deadly with buckshot or slugs at any substantial range.

David Holden kept to a crouch as he moved forward, closer to the rocks which the seven attackers had vacated seconds earlier. In seconds more, even the most dimwitted among them would detect that an arc of their circular formation was three men shy.

Time had run out.

Holden dropped to knees and bare elbows and settled into a prone position with the M-16 tucked into his shoulder cup. His thumb already had set the safety tumbler to auto. He could run for it, his immediate needs for ammunition, even transportation across the river, met.

Instead, David Holden opened fire directly in front of him, cutting down one of the remaining seven. He swung the muzzle right, cutting down one more of the men.

Assault rifle fire tore into the rocks near him, but Holden was up into a low crouch, already running with the M-16 at high port. Bullets whined and ricocheted off the rocks, ripping chunks out of the trees. He kept running, eyes squinted against the dust spray.

He reached the trees.

The revolver. He fired it indiscriminately as he ran toward the skirmish line, drawing fire to this new position, evacuating it before they fired.

He reached the far side of the circle. The entrance to the precariously balanced little house was directly before him and fewer than two hundred yards distant.

More shotgun fire blasted from the house.

A wave of answering fire blew the door of the house out. Holden had his rifle to his shoulder, firing out the magazine. The men of the skirmish line took cover in low bleached white rocks about seventy-five yards from the house. Holden's gunfire blew dust and rock chips over them, not striking them.

Holden saved the empty magazine, loading a fresh one up the magazine well as he ran. Doubling back along his earlier route, he changed positions again, loading the revolver two rounds at a time on the run. When he reached his earlier position, he fired out several shots, ran a few more yards, and emptied the revolver. He ran toward the position from which he had originally fired, the position vacated by the seventh man. He fired a series of rapid full-auto bursts from the M-16.

He ran now to the north, toward the direction from which the three men he had killed before the shooting began would have been coming had they survived to join the skirmish line.

He fired the last loads for the revolver. He fired another burst from the M-16. The idea, of course, was to make his adversaries assume that several men, well armed, were in turn surrounding them as they surrounded the house with the hapless shotgunner inside. When Holden reached the weakest area of the circular skirmish line, he stopped, fired a burst, changed magazines, and started downward. There was a defile, a stream course in wetter times or during flash floods, but now, a narrow bed of loose gravel and soft dirt, it was shielded from the height of the rocky hill.

He reached the end of the defile, where the sidewall vanished abruptly and the stream bed fanned outward only to dissipate several yards away. Holden veered left and dropped behind the cover of several large rocks.

He was a hundred yards from the house, half that distance from the nearest of the five remaining attackers.

He brought the M-16 to his shoulder, settling the sights as he thumbed the selector to semiauto. He fired once, the head of the man who was his target seeming to implode under the impact of the bullet, a wash of red on the air for an instant as Holden tucked back. With only one shot it was dubious if anyone had seen the position from which it was fired and, amid the general cacophony of the gun battle, even more doubtful anyone would have heard it at all, let alone clearly enough to have isolated the source.

Holden peered out from behind cover, the M-16's selector on auto again.

No gunfire was directed toward him. One of the remaining four men was running from rock clump to rock clump, trying to get off the slope to safety.

Holden edged outward slightly, ready to fire. But one of the three Hernandez men fired first, a full auto burst across the small of the man's back, nearly sawing the torso in two as the body flapped onto the ground and lay there.

Only three men left.

Holden edged back along the defile, to its approximate midway point, using his knife on the loose dirt of the side, pulling himself upward as he drove the knife downward. He reached the top.

David Holden threw the M-16 to his shoulder again. The Hernandez man who had shot the fleeing hireling was moving laterally along an aggregate of low rocks, firing toward the house as shotgun fire returned ineffectively. Holden fired a three-round burst, then another and another, the second and third burst connecting, twisting the Hernandez man's body around corkscrewlike. The M-16 in the man's hands discharged into the rocks on full auto, throwing up a cloud of rock chips and dust, the whining of the ricochets almost deafening.

Gunfire from the remaining two men poured up into the niche in the defile wall from which Holden fired. Holden skidded downward on his rear end, wiping the blade of his knife clean on his trouser leg as he reached the bottom. Then, sheathing the knife, he was up, moving again, upward along the defile. The roar of assault-rifle fire coming into the defile wall above him was intense, starting little rockslides everywhere as stray bul-

lets whined off rocks and debris, raining loose dirt
down on him.

He squinted his eyes against it.

At the height of the defile Holden made a tacti-
cal magazine change, then dropped to knees and
elbows, following the ground contour as he wrig-
gled toward cover under more assault-rifle fire and
an occasional pistol shot. The thirty-round magazine's spring died as Holden fired the first shot off
the top of the stick. "Shit!" As he withdrew the
magazine, the loose rounds beneath the stuck fol-
lower and set spring spilled from the feed lips to
the ground beside him.

Holden had the Beretta into his fist. There was
no time to reload a magazine now, because as he
peered over the rocks behind which he'd taken
cover, he could see the last two Hernandez men
charging his position. Each of them was armed
with an M-16 like the useless one beside him, one
of them holding a pistol as well. Holden had the
safety up and off, thumbing back the hammer for a
more accurate first shot. He fired, then again and
again and again, tucking back as the rocks beside
him seemed to explode under a hail of bullets. The
last image in his eyes was of one of the men—the
one with just the assault rifle—going down.

Holden used the Beretta's safety to drop the
hammer, then raised the safety to the firing position again. He rammed the pistol into his trouser
band. The M-16. He grabbed up one of the good
spent magazines from his liberated ditty bag,

cramming loose 5.56mm rounds beneath the feed lips and back, as rapidly as he could.

A half-loaded magazine. The sound of assault-rifle fire came from close range.

Holden was up, rolling to his right, ramming the magazine home as he came from behind cover, driving the bolt of the M-16 forward.

His right first finger found the trigger as the last Hernandez man, assault rifle and pistol blazing in his hands, came up over the natural rock wall, face bleeding, eyes aflame with hatred.

Holden's M-16 spit all ten rounds.

Holden rolled again, the Beretta in both hands, the double-action pull half finished. The Hernandez man's body froze.

The rifle tumbled from the Hernandez man's right hand.

"¡Hijo de puta!"

"Fuck you," Holden snapped, the trigger snapping back under pressure of his right first finger as the Hernandez man stabbed his pistol toward Holden's face.

Holden's Beretta fired first.

From a hole just over the right eye a wash of blood flowed across the bridge of his nose and over the eye as both eyes locked open and the man—he was already dead—fell back and down.

Holden rolled back to cover, taking the time to breathe.

The Beretta was in his right fist, the hammer still cocked, as Holden's left hand snaked out to grab for his rifle. He had it and drew it back behind the cover of the rocks.

A voice called over from the house. *"¿Quién es usted?"*

"Un amigo," Holden shouted back, his fingers already flying between the loose ammo in the ditty bag and the empty magazine.

"You don't sound right," a New York–accented voice came back.

"Yeah, well, maybe it's cause I'm not from Manhattan?" He had the magazine loaded, ramming it up the well, chambering the first round. He swapped magazines in the Beretta. "Who are you? What'd these assholes want?"

"Any fool could see that. They wanted to kill me!"

"No kidding," Holden called back, beginning to like the repartee. "Why? Your golden personality?"

"Who are you? Tell me first!"

Holden considered, shrugged his shoulders, and called back over the rocks, "I'm David Holden."

There was a moment of silence. "Nuts!"

"Fine; I'm the ghost of Elvis Presley, then. So, who the hell are you?"

"Anthony Bernardelli. I'm with—"

Holden finished it for him, "—Trans-America News World."

"Hey, hey! You can read!"

David Holden licked his lips, then stood up, the

61

rifle and the pistol in his hands, but his arms away from his body. "You got binoculars?"

"Yeah."

"Then look at my face," David Holden challenged.

Nothing. Silence.

And then he heard Bernardelli's voice. "Holy shit! Professor Holden! Here?"

David Holden lowered his arms slowly as he walked toward the remnants of the shot-up little house. "Do something dumb with that shotgun, Mr. Bernardelli, and I'll have to shoot you. Right?"

Bernardelli stepped out of the house, holding the shotgun by its muzzle in his left hand. He leaned it against the side of the house and walked forward, hands away from his sides. "What the hell is the hottest name on the Ten Most Wanted List doing in Peru?"

Holden had a flash of inspiration, smiling as he said, "Maybe the same thing the prizewinning journalist and syndicated columnist is doing in Peru, huh? Emiliano Ortega de Vasquez and Innocentio Hernandez, the FLNA, and the drug smugglers who finance it, huh? And next time, for pity's sake, get something more substantial than a shotgun, huh?"

Bernardelli stopped walking, started to laugh. "A point well taken. I never carried a gun in Vietnam. Figured I'd need one here and so I brought the thing along. Wild animals, I told myself."

David Holden stopped walking. He looked at

one of the dead Hernandez men near Bernardelli's feet. "Wild animals, huh? Well, I guess you were right about that, anyway."

Holden safed the Beretta and slipped it into his waistband, then took out the pack of Camels, pulled a cigarette out, and looked at Anthony Bernardelli. Bernardelli shrugged. "Gave it up."

"Me too," David Holden told him, lighting up with a dead man's cigarette lighter.

CHAPTER

10

Theron Hyde wasn't an operative, so Thomas Ashbrooke had not expected him to be drug resistant. And Hyde was not. Hyde didn't struggle as one of the sodium-based so-called truth serums was administered, cooperated nicely by counting backward from one hundred, and went under peacefully.

"Tell me your name," Saul Rothstein began.

"Theron Hyde."

"What is your occupation, Theron?"

"I broker arms transactions and drug transactions for the global terrorist network."

Thomas Ashbrooke listened to the faint hum of the tape recorder and the even fainter hum of the overhead fluorescent lighting. A bad ballast, he conjectured. He glanced at the tripod-mounted video camcorder and the Israeli agent behind it.

"What are the whereabouts of David Holden?" Saul Rothstein asked.

"He was with Ortega de Vasquez. Hernandez brought him there."

Thomas Ashbrooke shivered, even though it was so warm in the basement of the suburban London home, that he was in his shirtsleeves.

"Is David Holden dead?" Saul Rothstein asked.

"I don't know."

"He could still be with this"—Rothstein looked at the pad of the pretty girl beside him. She'd been taking notes on a steno pad and she quickly wrote something out for him— "with this Ortega de Vasquez and this Hernandez man?"

"Yes."

"Where would he be? Geographically."

"Peru."

Rothstein looked at one of the other Israelis. "Get me an atlas or something. Hurry, man!"

Thomas Ashbrooke closed his eyes, murmuring, "Thank God," under his breath. . . .

She'd gone to bed early, exhausted enough that she hoped to sleep. Suddenly, Patsy Alfredi had been in the tent, whispering, "Hey, Rosie. Mitch Diamond radioed us. That telephone call you were waiting for. That pay phone by the old stop-and-rob."

These days, the Patriots had their own sort of slang. David used to refer to it as "argot." It was a

65

mixture of cop talk, military stuff, and things out of movies. Stop-and-rob/convenience store.

She sat up. "Gimme that blouse," she told Patsy. . . .

She wore a skirt and no stockings and her legs were cold as she left the van and walked across the parking lot toward the telephone. The black briefcase with the telephone gadget was in her left hand. She was saying David's name under her breath, reciting it like some sort of mantra.

As she neared the telephone, it began to ring. She looked at the watch. She'd worn the Timex Ironman by mistake, which looked stupid with a skirt.

She answered the phone. "Hello?"

"Use the case."

"Nuts! Is he alive?"

"Yes, now use the case, damn it."

"Okay." She made the sign of the cross, then started figuring out again how to use the case, which was exceptionally hard at that moment since her eyes were filling with tears.

CHAPTER

11

"**D**on't bring any weapons. I'll supply whatever you need."

"One of the IMI Desert Eagle .44's. Trust me. There's just a reason for it. Please?"

Tom Ashbrooke—when had she started thinking of him as Tom instead of Thomas or Mr. Ashbrooke?—had told her, "Odd you should mention something Israeli. Yes. Don't worry."

She sat in the front passenger bucket seat opposite Patsy Alfredi. Patsy was driving the big Chevy Suburban like a bat out of hell, the moonlight through the pines shimmering, almost shuddering, like the effect of an old silent movie over the hood of the Suburban and the road ahead of it.

"I hope David comes back to you," Patsy Alfredi suddenly said, lighting a cigarette. "We've all been almost as worried about you as we have been for him. Know what I mean?"

"It shows that much, Patsy?"

"You two—like a coupla kids. Kinda nice."

Rose Shepherd felt like blushing, and in the darkness of the front seat Patsy wouldn't have seen her. Instead, she stared down into the shadows where her hands rested in her lap. "You know, I've never been out of the United States. I never, ahh—"

"It's spring down there, if I remember my geography and everything."

"Spring, huh? Yeah. You think—"

"I think it makes sense that if they took him out of the country alive it's because they wanted to keep him alive, right? I mean, doesn't that make sense to you?"

"Yeah. But, you know how I feel?"

"Me? Maybe."

Rose Shepherd lit a cigarette. "I never figured I'd—" She'd never been much for "girl talk," never had much chance for it as a cop's daughter, then a cop herself, and even less chance now she was some kind of guerilla fighter. "I love him."

"David loves you. You can see that in his eyes the way he looks at you, Rosie."

Rose exhaled smoke against the Suburban's windshield. She ached for David Holden. A spark flicked off the tip of her cigarette and she brushed her hands over her skirt to keep the spark from burning her clothes.

Peru. Spring there. Why was she shivering just thinking about it?

CHAPTER

12

The head of the Midwestern station sat at the wheel of his XJ–6, smoke drifting up almost lazily from the bowl of his pipe. "This Roy Dumbrowski chap. Well spoken of in the community. Regular attendee at the neighborhood Roman Catholic church. Sponsors a bowling team and a Little League baseball team. Married, but his wife was institutionalized with some mental problem. I'm still looking into that."

Geoffrey Kearney lit a cigarette, staring at the restaurant window across the street. There were some broken windows along the thoroughfare which cut like a slash across Chicago's famous South Side. Not far from here, just west of Chicago proper, Al Capone's gangsters had roamed freely and such colorful upholders of law and order as the almost mythic Eliot Ness had worked to bring them to book. Archer Avenue, as was obvious from looking at it and borne out by Phillip Carlysle's running, occasionally rambling narrative, was an interlocking infrastructure of old-world neighborhoods transplanted from almost every European country imaginable.

Most buildings had smashed or boarded-up windows, but those of the Roman Catholic church a few blocks down, and of Roy Dumbrowski's restaurant remained pristine.

"In just what sort of institution is Mrs. Dumbrowski, Carlysle?"

"Mental, old boy. Went barmy over something. But as I say, I should have that for you by mid-morning."

"How far away is this place? The mental institution."

"Northern suburban area. This time of night, I should think, not more than a two-hour drive, possibly less."

"Maybe the answers I want aren't here, Carlysle. Up to a bit of driving?"

"We go mucking about at some mental institution, old man, we might run afoul of the police, certainly private security."

Kearney inhaled on his cigarette. "You can stay in the car. Let's get out of here. I'll need my car. You can be the wheel man unless you don't care to."

"My assignment is to aid you. I'll do that right enough. But you may be barking up the wrong tree, Kearney."

"Hmm—well, so long as nothing barks back."

CHAPTER
13

David Holden sat at the wooden table, Anthony Bernardelli across from him. The Roman Catholic nun set down a plate of bread and a young girl of no more than twelve—Holden thought of his two daughters, dead—was placing a pitcher and two cups on the table.

The nun smiled. The little girl curtsied. They both left the room via the arched doorway.

"Father Carlos Montenegro invited me up here once before. Simple food, but it's good. And not even Ortega de Vasquez or Hernandez himself would dare hit a Catholic church."

Holden didn't put much stock in Ortega de Vasquez or Hernandez respecting the sanctity of a house of God or even that they would hold back simply out of fear of public opinion. But Bernardelli was right about the food. The beef was good and so was the bread—Holden made himself a sandwich Dagwood would have blushed at—and the red wine, a little resinous tasting, warmed the pit of his stomach.

They ate in silence for some time, Holden working on his second sandwich, pausing between bites of the sandwich and sips of the wine to ask, "So, why don't you break down and tell me? What's a big-time hotshot journalist like you doing down here?"

"You mean getting shot at by those Hernandez men? Easy. They figure maybe I know too much about their drug smuggling operation. And you know what?" He leaned back, fired a cigarette with a beaten-up nickel-finished wind lighter. "They're right. I've got tapes, times, some conversations—pictures." His eyes took on a hardness Holden hadn't seen there before. "They killed my cameraman, Harry. Slit his damn throat ear to ear, the fuckers," Bernardelli said, his voice sounding raw.

"Sorry." Holden nodded, sipping some more at his wine, trying to achieve a balance between satisfaction and inebriation. He decided to slow down on the wine before inebriation won. "So, then they came for you. Why didn't you get out?"

"I wanted more. Trouble with being a journalist. You always want more. Like being an alcoholic or a compulsive gambler—never enough. And, son of a gun, if I didn't meet the infamous Patriot leader Professor David Holden, right here in the middle of nowhere. So, what's the story, Doctor? Give it to me slow, 'cause I gotta remember it, unless I get up and get my notebook, and I'm too fuckin' tired to get up." He laughed.

Holden took another bite of his second sandwich, nearly finished with it. "I didn't exactly come here voluntarily, Bernardelli. A long story."

"Long stories can make great copy. How'd you like your side of the Patriot/FLNA thing told, huh? For an exclusive?"

"I don't see any other reporters around, man." Holden took another bite of his sandwich. He was starting to feel like he'd eaten too fast, which was probably an accurate assessment.

"No, I mean, once I spill it where you are, I mean even in general, every reporter in the USA's gonna be all over these hills lookin' for you. No extradition, huh? Too much heat Stateside so you're gonna fight from behind the lines? I mean, a lot of great patriots and leaders have done that, sort of like a government-in-exile thing, you know? Like de Gaulle during World War Two when things were run out of Vichy under the thumb of the Nazis. Like that?"

"No." It wasn't like that at all.

"I've been down here for three weeks. Missed the story on the President—"

"Is he still alive?" Holden interrupted, setting his cup down so violently, he spilled some of his wine.

"Yeah, if you call it living, I guess. Last I heard. But Roman Makowski's running the show now.

And he'll keep running it." Holden lit one of the captured cigarettes as Bernardelli kept talking. "Gonna make it hot for guys like you. That Makowski's got his own way of doing things, let me tell you, and it's his way or not at all. He was like that in the House all these years. Never made any bones about the reforms he wanted."

"The word *reform* implies that something was wrong to begin with," Holden volunteered.

"Missed the biggest story of the century, the phone company building getting hit in that rocket attack, the Vice President killed, the President nearly killed. That's why I've gotta make this drug thing pay off, so my editor stops shitting. And now with you, hey—that other thing would have been shared with every reporter in the world. But I've got you all to myself."

"You want the truth? Wonderful. We were given a tip that their other battery of missing antitank rockets was at an airfield. We went out to investigate and it was a trap. They nailed me—got some of our people—and the next thing I knew this Russian named Borsoi was using electric shock and ice-water drownings and abdominal beatings"— there was a twinge of pain as he remembered it, his own private sojourn in hell—"then I was drugged up and I woke up down here, the guest of Ortega de Vasquez. Hernandez was the one who brought me down here. He's still running around with my shoulder holster. I escaped."

"Man, you must be tougher than everybody

says. Hernandez is a heavy hitter. He used to work for one of the Five Families in New York City. An enforcer. They say he was responsible for the Albany Massacre."

Holden ran the name through his head. He had it. "That was the thing about five years ago—"

"Seven years ago last month. One of the rivals of Hernandez's boss was in Albany for his daughter's wedding. A group of hitters in ski masks walked in at the elevation of the Mass and killed twenty-six people, injured another dozen or so. That was when Hernandez hit the trail south of the border. He was even too hot for the mob people. Hernandez's boss supposedly said, 'Get so-and-so and I don't care how.' Like that. Never figured Hernandez would grease half the wedding party right in the middle of church."

"Innocentio Hernandez won't be 'greasing' too many more people. He doesn't have long left on this earth. Trust me on that, Bernardelli."

The newsman's eyes lit up. "Goin' after him? Vendetta of some kind?"

"Vengeance pretty well sums it up. The word *vendetta* has always implied an unreasoning hatred for a wrong done, while *vengeance* has always implied a more calculating attitude toward the thing. I'll call it 'vengeance.'"

CHAPTER

14

The name on Luther Steel's airline ticket had troubled him. He had no false ID, and although Rocky Saddler had volunteered to have some fabricated for him, aside from the delay such would have entailed, it irked him on a very personal level that an honest man, and an FBI agent at that, should have to travel under a false name to avoid assassination in the United States. He'd compromised, listing his occupation as an attorney (which he was, although he'd never practiced law). These days, there were identification forms to be filled out when airline tickets were picked up, and a photo ID had to be shown.

For those who did not drive, the government—then Speaker of the House Roman Makowski had sponsored the bill—required that Social Security cards of the conventional variety be replaced by photo-bearing ID cards. Suspiciously like a passport, Steel had thought at the time.

He had not shown his badge but his driver's license and new Social Security card instead.

And, he had traveled weaponless. Airline restrictions on transporting firearms as baggage were tightened to the point of impossibility, and without showing his badge, he could not carry aboard an aircraft.

At the dead center of the lower-level parking lot, a car started up and Steel froze. Although he had expected a car he had also expected that the engine wouldn't have been left running. Gasoline was harder to come by these days because so few service stations or convenience stores stayed open after dark, and confounding the situation still further, it was getting on toward winter and darkness came earlier.

Steel began walking again.

He felt his face seam with a smile. Bill Runningdeer stepped out of the car and into view. . . .

Clark Pietrowski drove, Tom LeFleur sat in the front passenger seat beside him, and Luther Steel, Bill Runningdeer, and Randy Blumenthal were in the rear seat. "I had to tell 'em I was you at the bank. Only way they let me into the safety deposit box. God, you've got a scrawly signature, boss."

Steel heard Blumenthal, the youngest of his men, stifle a laugh. Runningdeer handed over an attaché case and Steel put it on his lap, opening it. Inside was a SIG-Sauer P-226 identical to the one he'd left with his wife and children and Rocky Saddler, a DeSantis Slant Shoulder rig with an off-side double magazine pouch and several standard-length and twenty-round spare magazines. There were two green plastic MTM ammo boxes and, inside these, his personal favorite 9mm round, not the Bureau preference Federal 115-grain JHPs.

"Guess he figured two hundred rounds'd be enough for you for the time being." Clark Pietrowski laughed.

Steel began loading the pistol's magazines.

"Do you have a plan, Mr. Steel?" It was Randy Blumenthal who spoke.

Before Luther Steel could answer him, Tom LeFleur said, "Luther's always got a plan, man."

Pietrowski had them into the sparse late-evening traffic so easily, Steel barely noticed it.

Steel just looked at LeFleur and smiled, then turned to Blumenthal, telling the younger man, "As a matter of fact, I do, Randy. The five of us are are as good as dead unless we take one of the only two options I see left to us. And the second option is pretty radical. We've either got to crack this case wide open and fast or go underground and join the Patriots. We can't handle this alone."

"Join the Patriots—"

"We all have families. And, thank God, we all have places to send them to be safe until things normalize, however long that might be. And it could be a long time. We have to crack it or go deep. Otherwise, they'll get us one at a time. I don't think any of us look at the Patriots as law-breakers. They're good Americans trying to do what they think is right. So are we."

"What's the first option entail?" Runningdeer asked.

"I tell you, Bill, we may have had this right under our noses all along. What's the name Humphrey Hodges mean to you?"

Runningdeer paused for a moment, then answered, "He was department chairman at Thomas Jefferson University, where Professor Holden taught. He survived the graduation-exercise attack essentially unscathed. He took a leave of absence from his post to pursue independent research. Still lives in the Metro area."

"Remember one of the police reports from the assault on Cedar Ridge Islands? After the assault. We had the local cops running a list for us of any out-of-area license plates? And I remembered one of the license plates. It's not a prestige plate or anything, but just something that clicked mnemonically with me. It incorporated the last three digits of my wife's phone number before we were married. I'd seen that plate number before. It didn't hit me until the attack on the safe house. Tell them, Clark."

Clark Pietrowski powered down the window, snapped his cigarette butt into the night, then said, "That license plate—Humphrey Hodges's license plate—was not only at Cedar Ridge Islands just after the assault, but got an illegal parking ticket near Cedar Ridge Islands a couple of weeks before."

"Then Hodges could be a link to—"

Steel looked at Blumenthal. "If Borsoi didn't die, Hodges could be the link into the FLNA. That could explain how he survived the attack on the graduation exercises, why he was at Cedar Ridge Islands a few weeks before the attack and there in the aftermath. What if Borsoi/Johnson was banged up and needed a ride, needed a safe place to hide out? What if he called a man he'd worked with all the time but a man who was whistle clean? If Borsoi was hurt, he couldn't risk being caught with some of the Leopards street gang people in a stolen car. He'd need something legitimate. What if he called Humphrey Hodges?"

"We find out, right?" LeFleur asked, looking at Steel over the seat back.

"We find out." Luther Steel nodded. And if this didn't work, there wasn't any hope left at all.

CHAPTER

15

The wall rose upward some eight feet, in itself not anything to worry about. He'd always been athletic and this was barely an obstacle. At the height of the wall were strung several strands of barbed wire. He guessed these were electrified or at the least connected to an intruder system. Likewise, there were probably motion-sensitive switches on the grounds beyond the wall which would, through microwave transmission disruption, activate floodlights.

He looked at Carlysle. "Take off your jacket and your tie, would you? Then muss up your hair."

"What?"

"You said you'd help. We're trying to get into a mental institution, correct? So, if you look like a mental patient, we have a way in."

"You're insane. How will mussing my hair and going coatless make me appear deranged?"

Geoffrey Kearney smiled, saying, "Trust me, old man." Kearney stared out the Jaguar's window toward the main entrance. . . .

Beneath the jacket of the black suit, Kearney wore no weapons. But inside the little pocket at the wide end of his black silk knit tie, the black B & D Trading Fazendeiro folding knife was suspended. It weighed the tie down a bit, but was otherwise unnoticeable. They got out of the car. Kearney approached the gates almost towing Carlysle along. The resident agent's shirt was half out of his pants, one shoe missing, tie and belt gone, one trouser leg was bunched up over his calf as if he were readying himself to ride a bicycle.

Carlysle looked terrible, exactly the way Kearney wanted him to look.

"This isn't going to work, old man," Carlysle hissed under his breath.

"Only has to work well enough to get us inside. Rest easy."

At the driveway gates, only a few feet from the front of the Jaguar, there was a video camera and, beneath it, a squawk box. Almost slamming Carlysle against one of the gate pillars, Kearney thumbed down the button and said with his nastiest American accent, "Just who the hell is in charge of this place that your patients wind up wandering the roadsides trying to get a ride?"

He waited.

After so long a pause that he was tempted to talk

into the little box again, the camera mounted above it began to move, automatic focus grinding. A voice came back. "He isn't one—"

Kearney depressed the button several times to let the speaker know he wasn't interested in hearing what the man had to say. "Either open this damned gate and get me someone with some authority to talk with or I'm hauling this poor man off to the nearest police station and demanding a full investigation! Now, what's it going to be?"

There was a long pause again, then the same voice said, as the camera whirred and buzzed all the time, "Just a moment, please."

Carlysle slid down along the side of the pillar, legs folded Indian fashion, running his hands through his hair, looking for all the world as disoriented as a real mental patient might—just as Kearney had rehearsed it with him.

After a few moments a sleepy-sounding voice came over the squawk box. "I'm Dr. Lauren Bledsoe. That man with you is not one of our patients. I should know. I'm chief of staff."

Kearney suppressed a smile. "I'm Dr. Phillip Ridgeway." He had the identification papers to prove it. "And if this miserable fellow isn't one of yours, then you owe it to him as a doctor to get him someplace where he won't hurt himself—my God, I think he just soiled himself!—you owe it to him immediately. If you don't do something right now, I'll contact the state psychiatric board at once. I don't practice in this state, but believe me you'll learn I have connections."

"You're Dr. —"

"Phillip Ridgeway. With Boston College. I'm in Illinois on a personal matter visiting my brother. He's with the state's attorney's office." Kearney was embroidering a bit, but there was no way of checking the story immediately anyway. "Now—will you take this man off my hands at once, or do I have to explain to my brother—it's his wife's car I'm driving—why there are human fecal stains all over the seats of her Jaguar!"

"I'm afraid you'll have to be searched, Dr. Ridgeway. These are perilous times."

"I quite understand. Get someone out here at once." And Kearney looked down at Carlysle, who'd evidently fallen into the spirit of the thing, was making faces, even sucking at his thumb. Kearney could always pass off the fecal-incontinence story by saying that Carlysle had displayed the obvious signs of flatulence.

As two men in white tunics and white trousers rounded the bend in the driveway, Kearney bent to Carlysle to "examine" him, whispering, "Don't try anything heroic until I make my move. You're doing splendidly, by the way. I think I've seen you once at Old Vic."

"I feel bloody silly."

"Shh." Kearney stood, working to haul Carlysle —rubber legged—to his feet.

The gates opened behind him and Kearney

turned toward the orderlies. "Be gentle with him. Not his fault he's in such wretched condition."

"Yes, Doctor," the taller of the two men said. The other was black and built like a body builder.

"Should I bring my car?"

"Dr. Bledsoe asked if you'd walk up with us, Doctor. It's a very short distance."

"Right."

"The search, Doctor," the shorter, stockier man said.

"Yes." Kearney raised his arms away from his sides, the black man making a quick and relatively thorough search, totally ignoring the tie and the lock-blade Fazendeiro as Kearney had anticipated.

Gently enough, they got Carlysle to his feet, giving him a pat-down but avoiding any area near his rear end thanks to the incontinence story. Kearney almost wished he'd thought of that part of the story earlier. He could have smuggled in a gun.

The two men took Carlysle in tow, glancing back as Kearney fell in behind them.

The driveway was easily wide enough for two-way traffic, lined on both sides with an even hedgerow—bushes nearly denuded of their leaves.

As Kearney followed them into the bed of the driveway, the awareness of the building itself was immediate, unforgettable. Twin turretlike structures dominated a stone building of considerable size, the overall impression that of a lightly diminutive version of a castle.

Indeed, the stone steps were long, low, and rose toward an impressively ornate entrance. Upon the steps stood two women, one in nursing attire, the other in a silk ankle-length bathrobe with a shawl about her shoulders against the night's chill, and a man in sweater, slacks, and bedroom slippers. The light shining from inside the edifice bathed the steps and the two women and the man in its glow.

The man came down from the height of the steps as they neared him. He was about average height, not so much slightly built as wiry seeming.

"I'm Bledsoe," he said, extending his hand as Kearney ascended the steps.

"Phillip Ridgeway. A pleasure, even under the circumstances. Look, I'm sorry to have sounded a bit put out—" Bledsoe's handshake was cool, dry, firm. Kearney had learned years ago that the old thing about a man's handshake being an instant judge of character was lunacy. One of the most evil and viciously deceitful men he'd ever met had a handshake like a dry rock.

"Understandable."

Kearney smiled, looking up at the two women who had remained at the height of the steps. "The poor man was wandering into the road. I'll admit I was unnerved. I almost struck him." Kearney shook his head, looked at his hands, made them tremble a bit. "Wouldn't have anything about like coffee or anything."

"A drink?"

Kearney smiled, glanced at his watch. "Well, perhaps a very little one while we sort this out."

They started up the steps together, Carlysle all but disappeared inside. Kearney couldn't let him quite disappear.

"How did you know we were here?" Doctor Bledsoe asked.

"I'd heard of the work you do here with schizophrenics and had seen the sign down the road with the name. The name registered. I naturally assumed he was one of yours and then almost hitting him like that with my sister-in-law's Jaguar . . ." They were at the height of the steps. Carlysle, still in tow with the orderlies, was just inside.

Bledsoe began a round of introductions. "This is Eileen Stihler, head nurse." The woman in nurse's mufti smiled, not extending her hand. "And this is Dr. Helen Fletcher, one of the best people on our staff."

She extended her hand. Kearney took it. She was brunette, blue eyed and very pretty. Her smile looked sincere enough, but somehow she held back. "A pleasure to meet you, Dr. Ridgeway. I spent some time at Boston College. You don't remember me, I'm sure, but I was one of your most devoted listeners in that lecture series you did—but I can't remember the title. I feel so embarrassed."

Kearney smiled. "Neither can I. I've given so many lecture series. The topics, of course, remain fresh with me, but whatever snappy title gets put on the series just goes." And he still held her hand. "Perhaps it's a symptom of something"—and he laughed, propelling her through the doorway, letting go of her hand only once he was inside.

Carlysle was seated on a wooden bench near something which looked like a library charge desk, with the two orderlies on either side of him like bookends.

The head nurse said, "I've got someone checking with some of the other hospitals and institutions nearby to see if they have a missing patient. It could take a while, I'm afraid."

Helen Fletcher said, "Is that offer of a drink open to me, too, Lauren?"

Doctor Bledsoe smiled. "Certainly, dear." And he looked at the head nurse. "See to some medication for our guest," and he gestured toward Carlysle.

Kearney put a hand on the nurse's forearm. "I wouldn't. I got a full whiff of his breath when I dragged him into the car. Smelled as though he'd just been administered something a while ago. Maybe just keeping an eye on him might be sufficient for now."

"Yes, good idea. Our insurance man would like you." Bledsoe laughed.

Bledsoe turned into the corridor, past the bench, Carlysle outdoing himself looking at once befuddled and totally out of it. "Cheer up." Kearney smiled at him. "We'll have you out of here quick enough."

"You seem to genuinely care for his welfare," Helen Fletcher remarked as they followed after Bledsoe. "Your attitude toward patients was one of the things I found so riveting in your lecture, Dr. Ridgeway."

Kearney smiled and pressed her hand for a moment. "Call me Phillip."

"Phillip. Yes. It's hard to imagine—I mean, you are so, well, young looking for your age."

"Strict regimen of diet, exercise, and plenty of time in bed," Kearney told her.

They reached an office door, Bledsoe unlocking it. "Patients, you know," Bledsoe said, flipping the key ring in his hand like a coin. He reached through the open doorway and Kearney heard the sound of switches being flicked, then Bledsoe ushered them inside a smallish but adequate outer office with a secretarial desk, a computer, and file cabinets all quite neatly arranged. He led them across it and into an inner office—his, evidently. It was luxuriously paneled, with parquet floors accented by small Oriental rugs. The chairs, the sofa, and the desk chair and desk top were of matching deep maroon leather. There was a small bar and a professional-looking maroon leather couch. "I mentioned a drink. What would you like?"

"Ohh, a glass of Scotch, please, but a small one." He'd taught himself years ago never to call it whiskey outside Great Britain.

"Scotch it is. Sounds good. Helen?"

"Ohh, just a little, perhaps."

"Ice or water, Dr. Ridgeway?"

"A little water, please." He'd never gotten used to so much ice, for which Americans seemed to have such an abiding passion. As Bledsoe stepped behind the bar, Helen Fletcher sat down at the foot of the small professional couch. Kearney lit a cigarette, in the flame of his Zippo glancing down at the face of his Rolex. He was pushing it. Soon, the head nurse would have checked with all the nearby institutions—if she bothered at all—and found out there was no missing patient matching Carlysle's description. The computer would have the records on Mrs. Dumbrowski and why she was hospitalized, unless names and records were falsified. It was elaborate for a hunch play, this, but if the Dumbrowski brothers were in with the FLNA, then Mrs. Dumbrowski might have been hospitalized to keep her quiet.

Kearney accepted the Scotch, Bledsoe sipped at his, setting it down on the desk and saying, "Don't think me rude, but I'm going to check on what progress Miss Stihler is having."

"Let me know how the poor fellow's doing, would you?" Kearney asked.

"I'll be only a moment. Please, make yourself at home. And that includes the bar." And Bledsoe left.

Helen Fletcher stood up, approached Kearney,

and stopped less than a foot away from him. "Are you the police?"

"Multiple personality, do you mean? No—there's only one of me."

She didn't smile. "You're not Phillip Ridgeway. There is no Phillip Ridgeway at Boston College and hasn't been one in the last ten years. Don't talk too loudly; he may have the room bugged."

"Bugged? Ohh. Microphones? Probably the professional thing to do, these days, malpractice insurance what it is."

"If you're not the police, then are—"

"What?" Kearney asked her, grabbing hold of her arm as he exhaled smoke through his nostrils.

"Then are you FLNA?"

"Why would I be that?"

"They stay here, sometimes. I learned about it only a few weeks ago. I haven't been able to get away to do anything since. And the county sheriff's police must be in on it too."

"Do you have a guest here named Dumbrowski? Celia Dumbrowski?"

"Yes. But there's nothing wrong with her. She's the one who told me about the FLNA and I thought it was just a manifestation of the symptoms on her chart. But I realized she was telling the truth, that her husband and his brother had put her away here to shut her up. You—"

"What?" Kearney asked her, stubbing out his cigarette in Bledsoe's desk ashtray.

"Can you help me?"

Kearney looked around the room. If it was a setup, it was a very good one. "Only if you'll help me." He heard footsteps in the corridor through the open doors. Raising his voice, he said, "I think I would like just a pinch more, thanks," and he tipped the whiskey into the plant on the corner of the desk, untouched. He handed Helen Fletcher the empty glass. She just stared at her own glass, her hand trembling as she set it on the end of the desk beside Bledsoe's glass.

As Kearney turned toward the door, he switched the glasses, with the little hope that if something were wrong with the drinks Bledsoe would make the mistake of sipping from the wrong glass. It always worked in the movies.

Bledsoe stood in the doorway between the outer and inner office. He looked considerably taller, somehow. Kearney thought that maybe it had something to do with the gun in his right hand.

CHAPTER

16

It was the same sort of route the drug smugglers used, she realized, only in the reverse. Rather than being smuggled into the United States, Rose Shepherd was being smuggled out. At the small airfield where Patsy Alfredi had dropped her was a single-engine aircraft and hardly big enough to feel safe, she'd thought. The aircraft landed almost three hours later at a private airfield in Florida and she was met by a man who called himself "Raoul" and spoke English without the slightest discernible accent. He'd offered her coffee out of a Thermos, given her a place to sit down inside his Porsche 914, and apologized that there were no more comfortable facilities for her, but the other aircraft would not arrive for a little while yet.

"What do you do, Raoul?"

She stared through the window out onto the rain-slickened black tarmac of the runway, the rain-splotched window breaking up the light from the single yellow bulb near the hangar building and diffusing it into a wash over the entire windshield.

"Do, miss?"

"Yes. I mean, what, drugs, shit like that?"

"Miss!"

"Do. The airfield. This little sex machine here. Porsches aren't cheap. I mean, I'm not trying to be rude and maybe I am anyway, but, hey, just tryin' to pass some time."

Raoul cleared his throat, his voice sounding genuinely hurt. He told her, "I own a car dealership, miss. I am a Patriot. The airfield belongs to another Patriot—or, to his widow, I should say. He was killed."

Rose Shepherd felt like two cents. "I'm sorry. I was a cop, before all this, and the operation—"

Then Raoul laughed. "Yes. This was a drug-running route, more or less. The man who owned the field here, Billy Sage, was sure that drug smugglers were using it and he contacted the authorities. The police netted a lot of cocaine, but that was years ago. It is a logical place for jumping off to Latin America, miss."

"I guess so."

Rose Shepherd shut her big mouth and sipped at her coffee.

CHAPTER

17

Doctor Bledsoe evidently felt bigger with the gun in his hand, just sitting there all alone at the center of the sofa, the muzzle of the pistol aimed at Kearney's chest. He had summoned no help. Helen Fletcher still stood at the bar. Bledsoe spoke. "A normal man would have taken some of his drink. You didn't. And there is no escaped mental patient from around here. And certainly not one wearing three-hundred-dollar oxfords and sporting a manicure, like the man out there."

"He confided to me that it was a mental hospital that was quite exclusive and only catered to the very rich. Didn't I mention that? And the Scotch smelled cheap."

Bledsoe laughed. "Well, I figure that you're not a doctor." And he waved the pistol toward Helen Fletcher. "Which means either you were onto him and didn't have the chance to tell me, Helen, or you're with him. What is it?"

Helen Fletcher's pretty blue eyes darted to Kearney's face, then away. "There is no Dr. Ridgeway in psych at Boston. I guessed he was a fake."

"Good girl. I almost believe that. So, if you just stand right over there beside the bar until some friends of mine arrive, you'll probably get out of this all right."

"Gosh." Kearney smiled, he hoped ingenuously. "You're a real prince."

"Well, smart-ass, let's see how glib you are when the Dumbrowski brothers finish beating the shit out of you."

"The Dumbrowski brothers?"

Bledsoe smiled again. "FLNA. Ring a bell? My bet is you're a Federal agent of some sort and you happened onto the fact that Mrs. Dumbrowski was here and put two and two together."

"Did I get four?"

"Yes."

"Good! My parents always wanted me to do well with mathematics. Are the Dumbrowski brothers local FLNA leaders?"

Bledsoe smiled again. "What the hell does it matter? They control FLNA activities from Milwaukee all across northern Illinois, Indiana, and into southern Michigan."

"They must have a hell of a schedule," Kearney said sincerely. "And Mrs. Dumbrowski, I take it, wasn't sympathetic? She was just locked up."

"Roy should have killed her. He wouldn't do it, said he was sure she'd come around and realize he was doing what had to be done for them. I could have killed her, but then Roy and Dan—"

"The Dumbrowski brothers."

"They would have killed me. So, I kept her here."

"And here is?"

"A safe house—a way station, if you like. Ever since the government destroyed Cedar Ridge Islands, we've been a little slow here. But I understand things are going to pick up soon."

"May I smoke a cigarette?" Kearney asked.

"Move your hands the wrong way and this gun goes off."

"You mean, you don't have to pull the trigger? That's amazing," Kearney grinned. Slowly he took the brass Zippo and the package of Pall Malls from his pocket. He lit a cigarette, saying, "Forgive me for not offering you one, but I'm almost out."

"Bad for the health anyway."

"I agree. I've cut my consumption by more than half in the last year, actually. What's the latest word on Dimitri Borsoi, anyway? Alive or dead?"

Bledsoe noticeably sat up straighter in the sofa. "Then you admit who you are."

"I'm actually an agent for British Secret Intelligence, SIS we sometimes call it. And I'm here to kill Borsoi—I mean here in the United States, of course—or whoever the number-one man is. Is it Borsoi?"

Bledsoe's face hardened into a mask. "You're pretty damned open about it, Ridgeway."

"The name isn't Ridgeway. But that doesn't matter, really. Is Borsoi alive? Is he number one?"

Bledsoe smiled his smile again. "Ohh, he's alive, and if what you said is true, maybe the Dumbrowski brothers can ship you to him. I understand through the grapevine that he just had that Patriot son of a bitch Holden as a guest."

"David Holden, you mean."

"The David Holden, yes."

"Did he kill Holden?"

"No—now shut up."

"Where's he to be found, this Borsoi person?"

"Shut up, damn it."

Geoffrey Kearney snapped the cigarette butt into Bledsoe's face and shouted to Helen Fletcher as he moved, "Drop flat!"

Bledsoe screamed, but only for an instant. A shot came from Bledsoe's pistol and hit the desk, then another smashed into the bar mirror as Kearney pulled the Fazendeiro out and dived for Bledsoe on the sofa. There was no time for any fancy tricks, just to kill or be killed, because even if the Dumbrowski brothers were still more than an hour's drive away, there were attendants and perhaps a whole building full of FLNA personnel just outside down the corridor.

Kearney hit him standing, with such impact that he knocked Bledsoe back, flipping the sofa back as well. Kearney's right shoulder stung as if it had been hit with a sledgehammer. A shot. Kearney felt heat and then cold in his left thigh. As he fell crisscross on top of Bledsoe, Kearney raked the Fazendeiro deep across the inside of Bledsoe's right thigh, severing the femoral artery, then rolled back.

Bledsoe tried to stand, bringing the pistol up. As he took a step forward, his right leg buckled under him. He let out a single, choked scream; his eyes went wide and he was dead before he fell, the pistol discharging into the Oriental rug.

Kearney was on him within the same second with the Fazendeiro in his left hand, still open, Kearney's right hand wresting the pistol—it was a Walther P-5 9mm—from Bledsoe's dead fingers. Four shots were gone, leaving a maximum of five if the chamber was manually loaded rather than the first round stripped from the magazine.

No time to check.

The stocky black attendant was halfway across the outer office, a revolver in his right hand. Kearney shot him once. The body carried forward with momentum. When Kearney shot him again, the body slumped sideways, skidded, and stopped.

Kearney shouted to Helen Fletcher as he got to his feet, "Come along, Dr. Fletcher. Now's your chance!"

In the outer office Kearney wiped the Fazendeiro's large, single blade clean and did a one-handed closing of the knife, pocketing it. With his left hand he grabbed the dead attendant's revolver. It was a Smith & Wesson K-Frame with fixed sights and a bull barrel, the gap between the front face of the cylinder and the frame wide enough that it was probably just a .38 Special rather than a .357 Magnum.

"Who are you?"

It was Helen Fletcher's voice behind him. "Call me Geoff, all right?" There was a thermostat on the wall near the light switch. Kearney smiled. He turned it all the way down to four notches below fifty degrees Fahrenheit.

He didn't look back but into the corridor, where Carlysle was just about to have his brains bashed in with the .45 Colt automatic in the hand of the white orderly.

Kearney stabbed the Smith & Wesson revolver forward and fired as he shouted, "Look out, Carlysle!" Recoil bore out Kearney's assumption, it was just a .38. He fired again, both bullets smashed into the left side of the man with the .45. The man went down. Carlysle kicked the man in the face, stepping on the gun hand and tearing the pistol free.

"Out of here?"

"Not yet," Kearney shouted back. He turned and looked at Helen Fletcher. "Where's Mrs. Dumbrowski?"

"Second floor, all the way into the back. She's always sedated."

"Is the boiler on?" There were forced air outlets

and a return in Dr. Bledsoe's office, meaning oil or, more likely, natural gas. "Is it, woman?"

"It's been chilly the last few nights. I think so."

"The door there?"

"The door at the end of the hallway. But it's locked."

"I'll fix that."

Kearney offered Carlysle the revolver. "Four rounds left, I think. Get Mrs. Dumbrowski out of here."

Carlysle realized what Kearney was planning.

"But the other patients, man! My God, you can't!"

"The other patients are all FLNA, right?" And Kearney looked at Helen Fletcher. "Right?"

"Mrs. Dumbrowski and an old lady in the next room. She's been here forever and they didn't want to risk killing her, I guess."

"Get out any way you can," Kearney snapped, then shoved the revolver into Carlysle's hands and ran for it. "Be careful," he shouted behind him.

The basement door was locked. No time to play with it. Kearney took a step back and fired the Walther. The lock plate shattered.

He kicked the door at the lock plate. The door swung inward, half falling from the top hinge. There was a light switch. He hit it and there was light.

Inside the door was a long, narrow staircase. Kearney took the stairs quickly. There might not be the right things available to make the furnace blow the building quickly—he could always blow it if he had forever, of course—but a fast, small explosion and resultant fire would do the trick nicely. If an alarm sounded, police and fire personnel would arrive and those who escaped would be apprehended. If not, the FLNA's records wherever they cached emergency weapons, would all be destroyed.

At the base of the stairs he smelled it, an industrial-sized gas furnace.

He set about prying open the access plate at the front of the combustion chamber.

Patience.

In the far corner of the basement there were several cans of paint and wood stain and cans of stripping agent and turpentine, all safely stored on shelves. "Marvelous," Kearney said under his breath. He heard shots from above but ignored them; there was nothing he could do. The paint cans. He brought them beside the open access door, prying open the lids with the lip of the empty magazine from the Walther. Only one round remained, already chambered. He poured paint into the bottom of the access chamber, dribbling it everywhere, realizing that if he miscalculated he'd blow himself up.

He set the open cans, as many of them as he could, into the combustion chamber. He ran back, opened more cans, and positioned them as near to the combustion chamber as possible. It took three trips.

Kearney left the chamber door open.

The hot air distribution system ductwork was nearby. With the Fazendeiro, Kearney stabbed through the insulation-wrapped aluminum, cutting a ragged hole about six or seven inches in diameter. It would have to do. Making a mental note to touch up the blade of his knife on the ceramic sharpening sticks, he scanned the room. It was either find rags or use his jacket. No rags. "Damn." He stripped off his jacket, then his tie, almost ripping his shirt from his body. The shirt was more easily replaceable.

Kearney threw the shirt on the floor as he shrugged into his suit coat. He picked up a gallon of institutional-green paint and poured it over the shirt, leaving just enough of the shirt clean that he could pick it up. Kearney packed the shirt into the combustion chamber, very near but not touching the pilot light.

He started for the stairs, his left thigh not aching him so badly, just stinging. It had to be a grazing wound. He stopped in the shadows at the base of the stairs, tossing the empty magazine away.

Kearney started up the stairs.

More shots rang out, but this time from outside, which hopefully meant Carlysle, Helen Fletcher, the Dumbrowski woman, and the old female patient were outside.

Kearney stood at the head of the stairs, turned toward the furnace. He ran into the corridor, toward the still-open doorway into Bledsoe's outer office. He turned the thermostat all the way up, then ran. Aspiration, once the paint ignited, would suck the gas and flames through the small hole he'd made in the ductwork, taking the gas and flames everywhere throughout the building. He was fewer than six feet farther down the corridor when the explosion came, only shaking the floor slightly.

The flow of gas into the flames would keep the fire spreading.

Kearney ran along the corridor, throwing himself against the wall as searing hot flames leapt from an outlet duct.

He heard a scream. He ignored it. FLNA personnel would have to be staffing the place. The hell with them.

Kearney reached the front doorway, smoke already billowing upward from the basement stairwell as though the stairwell were a chimney, flames leaping up from the inlet ducts like gas jets.

He got to the front steps.

Helen Fletcher was down on her knees. Carlysle was firing into a knot of men coming square at him. There was the sound of a small explosion from behind him. Glass shattered above him.

Kearney raised his pistol and fired, killing one of the men with the last shot, then turning the pistol in his hand butt first, opening the Fazendeiro as he charged down the steps and into the driveway.

Three more of the FLNA personnel were down, but Carlysle was apparently out of ammunition and nearly out of steam. Carlysle held both pistols like hammers, backing up and taking a stand before Helen Fletcher. On the ground beside Dr. Fletcher was the emaciated form of an older woman, still in her nightgown and robe, as was Helen Fletcher. Dressed similarly to the old woman was a much younger woman, her dark hair in a ponytail and her hands over her eyes as she knelt on the ground.

Kearney charged the FLNA people from behind, crashing the pistol butt down on the back of one man's head near the nape of the neck, slashing the Fazendeiro across the left side of another man's throat.

A man grabbed at him. Kearney twisted half right with a double Tae Kwon Do kick with his left foot, delivering the first blow to the chest, the second to the groin. Kearney's left leg screamed at him with pain.

One of the FLNA people had a pistol. Kearney sidestepped, ducked, and raked the Fazendeiro upward along the man's testicles, rear to front. With the heel of his left hand—the P-5 was lost somewhere—Kearney smashed upward, into the base of the man's nose, breaking it, driving it upward through the ethmoid bone and into the brain.

The gun.

A Browning High Power, as the P-35 was called this side of the Atlantic. Kearney stabbed it forward as he thumbed down the safety and fired.

One man down shot in the face. Two more rounds, a double tap to another man's neck.

"Get the ladies out of here! Quickly!"

The last of the FLNA personnel were near to him. Kearney fired two shots into one man's chest and he was down.

The lower floor of the structure was on fire, flames leaping upward through a smashed-out window in the wake of a man diving through it, not quite quickly enough, his body overtaken by flames. He rolled on the ground. Kearney wasted a bullet and took him out of his misery. Flames were coming out of the upper-story windows now, but not the turretlike appendages at either side of the building. Perhaps no ductwork led to them.

More people were coming down the front steps, silhouetted in the glowing flames. Kearney squeezed off two shots, wounding one of them, blowing the glass out above the door with the second.

He turned and ran toward Carlysle, who was struggling ahead, Helen Fletcher helping him with the old woman. She was speaking incoherently. Stumbling along beside them was the woman with the ponytail, evidently Mrs. Dumbrowski, who was drugged or scared, or both, out of her mind.

The gates were closed and locked. Kearney grasped them and pulled.

"Stand back. Give me that empty pistol, Carlysle." Carlysle offered the Smith & Wesson revolver instead and Kearney took it, surrendering the 9mm he'd taken from the FLNA man he'd killed.

He started up the fence, realizing full well he'd never get the women over it. He smashed open the junction box for the electrical controls with the butt of the empty revolver, blood and hair still on it from when Carlysle had used it as a bludgeon. Kearney rammed the revolver's barrel between the wires to complete the circuit, almost falling as he sustained a mild shock. But the gate lock popped as the revolver fell to the ground.

Kearney swung his weight back as he dropped, swinging open the gate he clung to. Carlysle pushed the two women through, carrying the third.

Kearney ran for the Jaguar, taking the keys in his pocket. The spares were on a magnetized block stuck inside the wheel well just in case he'd been relieved of the primary ones.

He tore open the door and dropped behind the wheel with a quick glance to the backseat.

Kearney fired the ignition. Carlysle and the old woman were inside in back. Helen Fletcher pushed Mrs. Dumbrowski into the backseat, then dropped into the front seat beside him. "All right!"

Kearney stabbed the P-35 through his open window and fired it out, zigzagging the muzzle to right and left, then throwing the pistol to the ground. The Jaguar had an automatic transmission. He stomped the gas pedal and the Jaguar reversed fast.

Kearney shouted, "Hold on tightly!" He cut the wheel and engaged the emergency brake, the Jaguar spinning around a little more than one hundred eighty degrees. Kearney tapped the brake as he threw the shift into drive and stomped the gas pedal again. Bullets whined off the coachwork, shattering the mirror beside him.

"You did that! That fire and explosion."

Kearney looked at Helen Fletcher. "So?"

"How—how could you? They were the FLNA, but they were people. How—"

"It was very easy. I can show you how in about five minutes, if you're talking technique. If you aren't, don't talk to me about it at all. There's no question of morality here. Your little Front for the Liberation of North America is nothing more than a group of terrorist killers. They got what they give, Dr. Fletcher. End of subject."

Geoffrey Kearney was angry and he lit a cigarette, which if he didn't watch himself would put him over his quota for the day.

"Shit." He put the Jaguar's accelerator pedal flat to the floor.

CHAPTER
18

Anthony Bernardelli, for all his brashness, could not sleep soundly. He was actively dreaming and screaming and crying out in his dreams.

David Holden got up, naked except for a pair of clean underpants he'd borrowed from the priest, and walked to the door of the small room he shared with Bernardelli. "Go to sleep, Anthony," David told him, as reassuringly as he could, and Bernardelli turned over.

Holden went to the bed, picked up the blanket he'd had across him, and wrapped it around his shoulders, taking the Beretta pistol, the last of his stolen cigarettes, and the stolen lighter and walking out into the small corridor.

He walked toward the rectory porch, almost losing the blanket as he made for the gun, startled by a figure sitting on the front porch railing smoking a pipe. It was Father Carlos.

"Dr. Holden. You cannot sleep either."

"Ahh—"

"He did that the last time he was here. It was cruel of me to have the two of you share a room. Señor Bernardelli is very troubled in his sleep. Apparently he is not as confident as he seems when he is awake."

Father Carlos reminded David Holden of the character of the old mission padre in *The Lone Ranger,* except that he was younger. He wore the brown robe and biretta of the Franciscan missionary fathers, like the padre had, and his voice had the same calm, the same soothing serenity to it. "How can you live here?"

"I do not understand, señor."

"How can you live in a world like this, where Innocentio Hernandez and Ortega de Vasquez rule everyone's lives? I mean, they must. They have the power of life and death."

"I deal with life and death, but I also deal with the afterlife. I have spoken with Hernandez. He is in great fear for his soul, as well he should be. He refuses to make confession, but he gives safety to this church. I do not give in to him. He is afraid of me. I wish that he were not."

"He'll be dead."

"Killing is not the answer, Dr. Holden."

Holden drew the blanket around him against the night's cold and sat on the railing on the opposite side of the low steps. He bent to set his pistol on the porch floor beside his bare feet, then lit a cigarette, balancing the lighter and cigarettes on the rail. The smoke was warm in his lungs, a familiar feeling. "What is the answer, Father? I gave up a long time ago on trying to find it for myself. I'm waiting to be illuminated."

Father Carlos laughed. "Then you have come to the wrong man. I attempt to guide, in my own humble way. If I had all of the answers to all of the questions, I would perhaps be in the chair of the Holy Father"—and he crossed himself, then laughed. "If I thought I did, I might be God, or the devil. But I am none of the three. You don't have to be Catholic for me to hear you, here, or there." He nodded his head toward the small church building, about seventy-five yards behind them. "God knows no denomination, Dr. Holden."

"Does God want me to let vermin like Hernandez walk the earth?"

"Did God appoint you as the instrument of His wrath?"

Holden laughed, half choking on the cigarette smoke. "You have a good mind, Father."

"And so do you, I think, or you would never ask such questions to begin with, would you?"

"Touché."

"Indeed. Tell me, señor, will you feel better once you know your enemies are dead?"

"I have many enemies, Father Carlos."

"If they were all to die"—he smiled, his face only faintly visible in the mixture of moonlight and the glow from the bowl of his pipe—"would you be happy?"

"Would I be happy that men were dead? I don't think so. But I'm not happy now. In my country, men and women, very brave ones, fight and die and still the war we fight goes on, as if forever. Hernandez and Ortega de Vasquez supply the drugs which finance this war."

"But what will killing them cost you, cost your immortal soul, Dr. Holden?"

David Holden inhaled on the cigarette. "I don't know. It's hard to imagine it costing me more than I've already paid."

"I have read about you in the news magazines. Your wife and your son and your two daughters died as a result of this war which you now fight, did they not?"

He was suddenly hot and pushed the blanket down from around him to where it only covered his legs, should one of the women, one of the two sisters or the young girl, still be awake. "They did," Holden was barely able to whisper at last.

"Will the killing return them to you?"

"Will the killing prevent the deaths of other innocents like them, Father?"

Father Carlos laughed. "Logic. It defeats us all, does it not? But I remember a slogan from the pacifist movement of the nineteen sixties. 'What if they gave a war and nobody came?' I ask you that. Could you, through great courage, renounce your guns, like that one on the floor beside your feet,

113

and accept the Gospel of Love, and make others accept it by your example?"

David Holden considered Father Carlos's words. He asked, "Father, if Christ were walking down a roadway and saw a poor unfortunate person set upon by thieves and killers, would he have acted?"

Father Carlos said nothing.

"If these thieves and killers had, in their benightedness, failed to recognize and thence be awed by His Divinity, merely continued in the pursuit of their evil, would Christ have intervened? I don't mean summoning the wrath of God down upon them, but perhaps as a mortal man would?"

"There is nothing in Scripture which—"

"Well, what do you think?"

"I—"

"I don't presume to have the knowledge to formulate an opinion, either, but somehow I feel inside me that ultimate goodness cannot be blind to evil, and that God gave man the ability to perceive evil so that he might attempt to counteract it. This is the only way I know how, to fight. Forgive me, Father, for I have sinned, and am about to sin again. Maybe."

Holden snapped his cigarette into the night, picked up his pistol, his cigarettes, and lighter and stood up and walked back into the corridor toward the room where Anthony Bernardelli slept in hell.

CHAPTER
19

The hotel suite was air conditioned, but she was still hot. The night outside had been cool when they'd reached the airport; but in here, with all of them, it was hot. A gooseneck lamp was over the table around which the men stood. There was one other woman, besides herself, an auburn-haired girl of maybe twenty-six. She wore khaki bush shorts and a hot-pink lightweight cotton sweater. She was sitting in the corner, smoking a cigarette. "First the equipment," the tall, blond-haired Israeli began. "I understand, miss, that you asked for one of the Desert Eagle pistols in .44 Magnum?"

"Yes. But not for me. I want to bring it along, give it to David. Do you have it?"

"Yes. I'd thought it was a bit too much for a woman; no offense, of course." He looked away awkwardly. She stared at him.

Tom Ashbrooke spoke after clearing his throat.

"For the rest of us there are enough Glock-17 9mms to go around, as well as an ample supply of nineteen-round extension magazines. But like as not, the submachine guns will get the bulk of the wear and tear on this operation. Uzis, of course. There's one sniper rifle available if it's needed, the old standby Steyr-Mannlicher SSG in 7.62mm NATO. We have sound and light grenades, of course, as well as C-4 for demolitions afterward. We don't want to leave anyone behind to interfere with our extraction and no one is going to want to come back here to finish the job."

"What about knives?" Rose Shepherd asked. She guessed she'd been hanging around David too long, and she smiled at the thought of that. *Too long* and *David's company* were mutually exclusive terms.

The young Israeli, leader of the commando team, answered her question. "Glock 81's with the hundred millimeters of sawteeth on the spine and Glock 78's with the plain spines."

She'd never seen one of the Glock knives, and apparently she conveyed that impression with her eyes. The Israeli reached under his khaki bush jacket, she heard a snapping sound, and a black-bladed, almost stiletto-shaped knife with a slightly Bowie-like recurve appeared in his hand. He rolled the knife, pommel toward her. This was evidently one of the 78's, no sawteeth. The Israeli said, "They're balanced for throwing, if you know how." She wasn't going to tell him that she didn't, but managed a nice roll of the knife to present it to him butt forward.

"The compound," Tom Ashbrooke began, the Israeli making his knife disappear, "has to be divided into two sectors for the sake of our attack. There's the outer area where Innocentio Hernandez's people live in barrackslike structures. Then there's the wall, beyond that the estate Emiliano Ortega de Vasquez occupies, quite plush and, supposedly, not well guarded, especially once the barracks area surrounding it is neutralized."

Rose Shepherd dug her hands into the pockets of her skirt, found her cigarettes and her lighter, lit one, sat down, and listened as the men kept talking.

Tom Ashbrooke was saying, "We can't hit the house until we're sure where he is, and the problem, of course, is getting around the barracks area surrounding it quickly enough that wherever David is, he isn't liquidated as a precaution."

"I am aware of that, sir," the young Israeli—he was good looking, kind of the Paul Newman type, minus the blue eyes—said back. "A soft penetration, as it is called, could give us his location. That is the only way."

"Excuse me?"

The young Israeli turned and looked at her, backlit by the yellow bulb from the gooseneck lamp which shone over the camp table on which the maps were being spread. "Yes, miss?"

117

"Soft penetrations don't make it in, pal. We hit them once and we hit so hard we can't help but make it in. That's how we get David. Somebody gets inside the compound first and figures out where he is, then, when the rest come in, leads them to him. We try going in and going out just to go in again, they'll be wise to us and David gets killed. No dice. None of this soft-penetration shit."

"Miss, you are obviously very distraught."

"I'm distraught, all right. And I'm gettin' real pissed off being a coupla miles from where David Holden is and sitting here listening to you guys chatter like you'd probably say women do. No. I can get inside. I can get inside and find David. I can lead you to him. Because I don't have anything to lose if David doesn't make it out. Nothing at all."

The Israeli laughed. "But how can one person get inside?"

At least he hadn't called her a "woman," a person instead. "Because I'm me. Those schmucks want me almost as bad as David. And if they've got David, and he isn't cooperating—and he won't be unless they're using enough drugs to fry his brain—then they can use me to pressure David. I'm safe as church—or synagogue to you—and once I'm inside I pull somebody's plug and find David and whistle for you guys. He's David. I'm the sling. You guys are the rock and this Hernandez son of a bitch is Goliath."

Rose Shepherd stood up, stubbed out her cigarette under her heel, and walked out of the room. As she passed the Israeli girl, Rose Shepherd got a thumbs-up sign and a smile.

CHAPTER

20

Luther Steel sometimes wished that he smoked. Health concerns regarding smoking aside, smoking had to make stakeout duties easier, more bearable. Just because it was something to do besides sip at cold coffee that hadn't tasted that terrific when it was hot.

Humphrey Hodges's car hadn't moved from the driveway. Steel could read the last few digits clearly. He had remembered them as part of his wife's telephone number in the days when they had been going together before they were married. Now, all the numbers did when he saw them was make him think of his wife, make him feel the loneliness more deeply than he already felt it, the loneliness intensified because of the brief moments of peace they'd shared before the attack on the safe house.

"I miss you."

"What?"

He looked at Bill Runningdeer. "I was thinking of something else, Bill. I wasn't talking to you, sorry. This duty's getting to me, I guess."

"Okay," Runningdeer said, then, after a long pause, asked, "You think this Hodges character's ever going to go anywhere or just sit here until we all die of old age or run out of patience or the cars rust away to dust?"

"We can only wait and see," Luther Steel advised, forcing a smile he didn't feel. "We know he's in the house, and if he is our man, he's got to move to make contact sometime."

"Be terrific if we had a wire on him."

"We'd need a court order and with our current less-than-legal status we'd be lucky if we didn't get clapped in jail for our troubles."

"We could do it without a court order."

"And anything we'd get would be inadmissible. Remember, we're out to arrest these guys, not kill them."

Bill Runningdeer groaned and looked away. . . .

He finally got to sleep, having dozed on and off through the night until well past two A.M. when, at long last, Bernardelli seemed to pass out of active dreaming. Had Father Carlos put him in the same room with Anthony Bernardelli to serve as a tangible reminder of what conscience could do to a man?

David Holden awakened late, a little past eight from the face of his Rolex, his mouth dry from too many cigarettes. Bernardelli was still asleep.

Holden shot him the finger, skinned into his pants, such as they were, and wandered down the rectory hallway. There was a solitary bathroom in the structure and it wasn't in use. He put the Beretta on the toilet lid, saw to his bodily functions, then took a towel and stripped, entering the metal stall shower. The water pressure was satisfactory, but the water was poorly heated. Regardless, he stayed under the water until he was numbed by it.

When he stepped out of the shower, fresh clothing—a white cotton sweater, a pair of faded blue jeans, clean underpants and socks and a handkerchief—was waiting for him. He dressed, balled up his old clothes. He smiled at himself to think someone had entered the bathroom, left the clothing, and he'd remained oblivious. A fat lot of good the gun on the toilet flush tank would have done him.

He put on the borrowed track shoes— Bernardelli's dead photographer had left them behind at the little house—and stuffed the Beretta under the sweater, into his trouser band.

Holden walked along the corridor again, the dirty wash left with the still sleeping Bernardelli. In the small dining area he saw Father Carlos drinking coffee from a china cup. "Have some coffee, Professor Holden. Did you at last sleep?"

"Yes, thanks. And thanks for the clothes."

Father Carlos smiled. "Sister Mary Lawrence

got them for you, but made me put them into the bathroom."

"You're very quiet."

"Yes, I saw your gun."

"I must have been more bleary eyed than I thought, not to hear you."

Father Carlos looked at his coffee. He spoke as though talking to it. "I was a member of what you might call a special forces or ranger group, before entering the priesthood. I learned to move silently. I'm sorry if it unnerved you."

"Is that why you spoke with such authority last evening?"

Father Carlos laughed, then abruptly stopped. "Authority, no. Experience, yes. One day, if you do not give this up, your sleep will be like that of Mr. Bernardelli, only for different reasons. He is not a brave man, like you, only brash. And you will have different dreams than he, but they will possess you as they possess him. I, too, am possessed by dreams."

Holden sat down at the far end of the table. Father Carlos stood up, got a cup and saucer for him, and poured him a cup of coffee. "We ate our breakfast several hours ago, but I can have food prepared for you."

"Coffee's fine. I ate enough last night to last me for two days." Holden looked at the coffee, wanted a cigarette, and was just as glad he didn't have them with him. He was nearly out, anyway. "So, you became a priest to atone for what you'd done? Is that the message you're giving me?"

"I answered what I feel was a call from God, to serve Him and His people. I can never atone for what I have done, not in this life. No one gave me the right to take human life, but I did so."

"Bernardelli wants to come with me, to get a story. He's even got one of his dead friend's cameras. I'd appreciate it if you'd find a way of keeping him here. He'd only get in the way and get himself killed in the process."

"You do not wish to have his death on your conscience, then."

"If you put it that way, Father, I suppose not." Holden nodded, sipping at his coffee. "I'll never be able to repay your kindness, but I realize you don't expect me to. You and the sisters and the little girl, you've all set a fine example of Christian brotherhood and charity. And I thank you for it. No matter what happens, I'll never forget that."

"And no matter what happens, you will never bring back your dead loved ones by more killing. I tried that myself. All that happened was that I died inside."

"I see your logic, but I have to do what I have to do."

Father Carlos smiled, sipped at his coffee. "A line from an American cowboy film, perhaps?"

Holden grinned at him. " 'A man's gotta do what a man's gotta do, Padre,' " Holden said in his best John Wayne voice, and it wasn't very good.

"Then may God grant you more wisdom, so you may more accurately perceive your duty in this world and prepare for your entry into the next."

"I hope you're right—about a next world, I mean. I'm in love with this woman, named Rosie Shepherd. And I still love my dead wife. I always will. I think Rosie and my wife, Elizabeth, would have liked each other. They're totally different. But still—Anyway, I hope you're right. I'd like to see my wife and children again. But, maybe if you're right, I'll be in the other place."

"I hope you find your way to them. I will pray that you do."

"I'll be leaving in a little bit. I'm going to scuttle one of the two boats on this side of the river, so Bernardelli can't follow after me too easily. Send him home, if you can. He's a creep but he's okay, I guess. Tell him that if I get out of this alive, I'll try to send him a letter or something and tell him what happened, so he'll get his story anyway. Okay?"

"Yes. I will do that. And if you should not, this woman you mentioned?"

"There's no way you can write to her, Father, not without compromising yourself. But if someday you should come in contact with her, well—you tell her what I said about her, please. And she'd understand."

Father Carlos merely nodded.

CHAPTER

21

Humphrey Hodges's car left the driveway just after dawn. Bill Runningdeer drove as Luther Steel ran the electric shaver over his cheeks and chin and neck and upper lip. Hodges was alone in the car, hopefully going to meet someone in the FLNA organization; and, if Dimitri Borsoi, the elusive Mr. Johnson, were still alive as circumstances suggested, maybe it would be him.

Steel put down the razor, his skin burning slightly. He picked up the walkie-talkie from the seat beside him. Conventional communications could no longer be trusted and the CB communicators, an idea borrowed from the Patriots, were the best alternative. "Bloodhound Two, this is Bloodhound One. Do you copy? Over."

Clark Pietrowski's voice came back. "This is Bloodhound Two. Reading you just fine, Bloodhound One. Over."

"Make the pickup, Bloodhound Two. I say again, make the pickup. Over."

"I copy that. Bloodhound Two, Out."

As long as one of Steel's chase cars had the Hodges vehicle in sight, any of the other two—the one driven by Pietrowski or the one with LeFleur and Blumenthal—could pick up the tail as the previous vehicle pulled off. If Hodges were watching for a tail, with any luck by the time he got suspicious, the questionable car would have disappeared, replaced by another.

Luther Steel smiled for a moment, starting to laugh. "What's so funny, Luther?"

Steel was laughing out loud now. "I just remembered something I hadn't thought of for years. When I was first out of the academy, right? This guy Max Terhune was organizing a three-car surveillance on a subject suspected of being involved in a securities theft. Terhune thought of everything, a classic three-car surveillance. But he was so busy with the details that he forgot the obvious. All three of the pursuit cars were the same color and make, so when one changed off and the next took over, the guy they were following couldn't tell the difference, thought the same car was following him all the time. I tried to tell him, but he wouldn't listen."

"Shit—what a stupwad!"

"Yeah, good old Max." Steel grinned. "They got him in personnel now, last I heard."

Runningdeer turned off into a convenience-store parking lot. Pietrowski's car turned into the street just as Hodges's car crossed the intersection.

"So far, so good," Bill Runningdeer remarked.

"Amen."

CHAPTER

22

David Holden stood under the roof of the lean-to outside the small garage. He'd stored his weapons there after reaching the church with Bernardelli. After the battle near Bernardelli's small house, there had been a considerable store of personal weapons from which to choose. Three of the M-16's were well maintained and in fine condition. Another Beretta, identical to the one he'd previously liberated. He had sorted through the weapons and other items of individual equipment while still at the house, unable to take everything, taking only the best. He inventoried the cache. A total of four M-16's. Two Beretta 92F 9mms. A Leatherman Tool, like his own which had been lost to him when he was captured. A GI pistol belt and two Bianchi M-12 holsters. One of these Holden had already converted from right-handed to left-handed use so he could carry one of the pistols on each side. Two serviceable musette bags in which he carried odds and ends. A magazine bag for the M-16's.

No combat boots.

The borrowed track shoes would have to do.

The sun was warm and nearly to its zenith as David Holden buckled on his gunbelt. A sheath from one of the dead men's knives nearly fit his knife and this went on the pistol belt as well.

A Remington 870 Wingmaster police shotgun.

Holden slung the M-16's, two on each side. It was oppressively heavy and awkward to carry them that way, but it was necessary.

With the police shotgun in his left hand Holden caught up the canteen he'd gotten from Bernardelli. It had belonged to the dead photographer.

David Holden looked back at Father Carlos's church.

And then he walked away. . . .

At the river, with the butt of the shotgun, he stove in a portion of hull on one of the Porta-Boats.

He left the boat in the open, going down to the other one which he'd already slipped into the water.

The rifles he'd already placed in the boat were joined by the shotgun. Holden took off his shoes and threw them into the boat, then pushed off the river's edge, his trouser legs rolled up, his pants barely getting wet at the bottom as he clambered inside.

He took up the oars, determined to use them rather than the small outboard. The outboard would be for emergency use only, too noisy to use otherwise.

He dipped both oars into the water and pulled.

There was something fresh in the air. An almost cool breeze blew over the water.

He kept rowing.

Reach the other side. Make it to Ortega de Vasquez's house. Kill as many of them as possible and, if you're alive, escape.

He wished he had explosives, but perhaps he could avail himself of Ortega de Vasquez's and Hernandez's hospitality and steal some to use against them.

He kept rowing.

He would have to get through the compound first, and night would be best for a variety of reasons. With any luck the two men he wanted most to kill would be together, in the main house.

"With any luck," Holden murmured to the wind.

CHAPTER

23

For some reason she wore the nicest clothes she'd brought with her. A cotton khaki skirt, full and almost to her ankles, and a navy-blue, sleeveless cotton sweater. Rose Shepherd entered the hotel bar and saw Tom Ashbrooke at once. He was a good-looking man, enough like an older version of David to have been his father instead of his father-in-law. He was sitting on a stool at a small table and waved when he saw her.

She smiled at him, stuffed her hands into her pockets, and walked toward his table.

He stood up. She sat down on the stool opposite him. Maybe that had always been part of her problem, being too good at sitting on barstools to be taken seriously as a woman. She mentally shrugged her shoulders. "Thanks for coming, Rosie."

"A good drink might help, anyway," she told

him. She looked at the watch on her wrist. The aircraft would be leaving in a little over an hour.

"I wanted to talk you out of going in there ahead of us, but for wholly practical reasons."

"You won't talk me out of it, Tom." She took her cigarettes from her pocket and before she could fire her lighter, Tom Ashbrooke had fired his and was lighting the cigarette for her.

"What would you like to drink?"

"Ohh, I'll be daring—make it a rum and Coke."

"Good choice. They used to call them 'cuba libres' before Cuba went communist." He slipped off the stool, went to the bar, exchanged a few knowing glances with the man as he spoke, then returned to the table. "I told the bartender to use the Myers Dark and real Coca-Cola. They're best that way, trust me."

"Did you tell him to slip a Mickey Finn in my drink too? I mean, not that your intentions would be dishonorable, but just so I couldn't do what I intend to do?"

Tom Ashbrooke laughed. The bartender brought the drinks. There was a slice of lime on the lip of the glass. She took it off, tasted at it with her tongue, set it on the napkin coaster beside the glass.

Tom Ashbrooke raised his glass. "To success."

"To David's being alive and free."

"Here, here."

They drank. The rum and Coke—cuba libre—

she wanted to make herself remember that term for some reason—was delicious.

"I have one rational argument for you, and since I know you're a rational person, even though you're acting out of love, I'll assume you'll buy the efficacy of my argument, Rosie. You won't be able to deny it. And then it's up to you, whether you value David's life over your ego."

"Men have egos, remember? I'm just a woman. All I have is gut-level reactions."

"And how about logic?" Tom Ashbrooke asked her.

"Sometimes." She smiled, sipping at her drink again, then took a last drag on her cigarette before stubbing it out.

"Maybe this will be one of those sometimes, then." Tom smiled. "Plain and simple. If you go in ahead of us and purposely let yourself be noticed, fine. Assuming you're as good as everything about you seems to spell out, you'll locate David and home us in. Problem is, whether you're as good as you seem to be or not, whatever happens, you'll alert the people in the compound to the fact that we know where they are and that they have David. Even if that doesn't jeopardize David's life, it'll make penetration of the compound exceedingly more difficult than it would have been.

"Now, my friends," Tom Ashbrooke continued, obviously alluding to the Israelis, "did me another service. You see, years ago when they were just getting started, before you were born, I did them a few favors. They have kindly tried to repay me by helping out with this operation. They did an over-flight and I've got aerial recon pix of the entire compound. We can study those, pick the likely places where David would be held and get in, get out, blow the compound. But if you go in first, they'll be waiting for an attack. It'll cost a lot of lives that might not have been sacrificed. I've got nine men and a woman, plus you and me. Twelve good people—and I'll admit I'm kind of rusty at this sort of thing—but we can do it, if we have surprise on our side."

"So, for slightly improving the chances of finding David unharmed, I might blow the whole operation and get David and a lot of other people killed? That's what you're saying?"

"That's what I'm saying," Tom told her. "I won't tell you that you can't go, but sometimes attacking a problem differently than one immediately proposes to attack it is hard to accept, is hard for the ego. Women have them. I know from years of experience. Do you want some time to make up your mind, Rosie?"

"My mind's made up." She sipped at her drink. The corners of his mouth downturned.

"I'm sorry you—"

"I'll wait and go in with you. But just hope to God you're right, Tom."

Tom Ashbrooke reached across the table and squeezed her hand. She couldn't look into his eyes, simply stared at her drink. She felt like her cheeks were on fire and her eyes burned.

CHAPTER

24

Humphrey Hodges changed cars in a self-serve multilevel parking garage in downtown Metro and continued driving. Luther Steel realized he was getting more cautious.

Randy Blumenthal and Tom LeFleur had just rotated off and Steel and Runningdeer were on.

The new car Hodges drove was a late-model Volvo sedan, easily capable of outdistancing any of the surveillance cars if it came to a chase, as none of the surveillance cars was equipped with an interceptor engine.

The blue Volvo was heading southeast on open roadway and a trailing car would be easier to spot.

"You thinking what I'm thinking, Luther?"

Steel nodded, saying, "We'd better change off cars more often to avoid his noticing us. Too little traffic out here and too much daylight."

"Got that right. Where the hell's he going?"

Steel grinned, saying, "If we knew that, all of this would be unnecessary, wouldn't it?"

Runningdeer kept driving. The night of sleeping in fits and starts in his clothes in the front seat of a car was beginning to tell on Luther Steel. And on Runningdeer as well. He imagined it was the same with the three other men. He rolled down a window, letting the slipstream pummel his face, to wake him up. It didn't help much. Tired men made mistakes too easily, Steel reminded himself. But there was no choice.

He wondered if Humphrey Hodges had had a good night's sleep, and bet with himself that Hodges had.

The Volvo started to slow at an intersection with a country two-lane ahead. "Shit," Runningdeer snarled.

Luther Steel got on the walkie-talkie. "Bloodhound Two, this is Bloodhound One. Come back fast. Over."

"This is Bloodhound Two," Clark Pietrowski came back. "Over."

"He's turning off just ahead of our position. You copy it? Over."

"I'll be on him, boss. Bloodhound Two out."

"Drive past," Steel told Bill Runningdeer, following the blue Volvo with his eyes. . . .

"My husband is one of the top men in the Front for the Liberation of North America. At first I thought it had to be some kind of mistake. I mean,

137

didn't it? I went to high school with Roy. He was on the football team. He was a regular guy. I mean, how could he be a communist or something?"

Helen Fletcher said, "Take it easy, Mrs. Dumbrowski."

"He couldn't find me here, could he?"

Geoffrey Kearney lied, "Of course not, Mrs. Dumbrowski. Tell us more, please." He lit a cigarette.

The air in the basement smelled damp.

She sniffed back a tear—she'd cried uncontrollably as the medication had started to wear off—and said, "He told me he had the good of the American people at heart, that our system was corrupt. I told him, he did pretty well in the system. We were making good money off the restaurant. It was hard work lots of times, but—He just wouldn't listen. We started shouting at one another. I don't know who started it. But Roy told me I'd better keep my mouth shut about it because Dan—that's his brother—because Dan had never trusted me and'd kill me as soon as look at me. Well, I started crying—" And she started crying.

Helen Fletcher moved from the straight-back folding chair on which she sat beside the card table and stood beside Mrs. Dumbrowski, comforting her.

Kearney shifted his weight and walked away from the doorjamb against which he'd been leaning, taking the stairs up two at a time, entering the kitchen.

Carlysle's wife, Melanie, was standing by the stove. Carlysle, in fresh clothes and looking more his dignified self, was filling his pipe from a pigskin pouch. The house, owned by a dummy corporation and rarely occupied, was used as a safe house only occasionally, and the rest of the time as a spot for a little R & R for British agents working anywhere in the vicinity who needed it. Not that active espionage was carried out against the United States, certainly in this century. But at times a British agent might be pursuing something wholly British which would bring him into the United States. Telling the Americans about it, if possible, was matter of course. Sometimes, such wasn't possible at all.

Kearney walked to the kitchen sink, looking out through the window over it at the pine trees that were all he could see in the darkness beyond the yard with the intermittent moonlight. He didn't like safe houses, because the very name implied somehow that one should let down one's guard and be foolish.

Mrs. Carlysle was making steak and eggs. The dishwasher was humming away on the drying cycle. The little house, easily cleaned, was more or less spotless, Mrs. Carlysle having reached it a few hours before Kearney and her husband had reached it with the women. The old woman was upstairs, sedated by Dr. Fletcher. She would have to be dealt with, suitable institutional accommodations found for her where she would be treated with dignity and kindness. She was old enough to be grandmother to everyone in the house, even Carlysle, the oldest of them.

"So, old man, feeling a bit less on the prod?"

Kearney flicked ashes from his cigarette into the sink. They made a hissing sound. For some reason Carlysle was looking at the Smith & Wesson automatic Kearney wore. "Why do you ask?"

"I've never been too terribly fond of guns, really."

"I've never been too terribly fond of being without one," Kearney told him. The truth to tell, Kearney realized that if someone with the FLNA knew about the safe house, it would be the first place the Dumbrowski brothers would come looking for Roy Dumbrowski's wife. And it was essentially indefensible. "Where's your gun?"

Melanie Carlysle looked at Kearney, then at her husband. "In the car," Carlysle said, almost embarrassedly.

"Won't do us much good in there, will it?" There was an ashtray on the kitchen table. Kearney stubbed out his cigarette in it. "I'm taking a walk around." Kearney left the kitchen, went into the small living room, and grabbed up the brown goatskin A-2 off the couch, pulling it on over the black cotton fatigue sweater. The sweater was bunched back so the butt of his pistol was more easily accessible. He left the bomber jacket open for the same reason.

Outside, the early evening air was cool and good to smell.

He heard the door opening behind him, turned toward the sound but, as he suspected, it was Carlysle, going out to the garage for the gun he'd left in the Jaguar. The Jaguar and the Ford with its Texas plates were parked in the structure. The little Honda Accord Mrs. Carlysle had driven to the safe house was parked in the driveway.

The cover story with the house was that it was a little retreat owned by a rich man and loaned out occasionally to his bizarre collection of friends. Hence, the little house was very luxuriously appointed with the latest electronic gimcrackery, an outrageous waterbed in each of the three bedrooms, real leather furniture, and the like.

Current accommodations were pressed beyond the max, however, the mentally ill old woman needing a room of her own, of course, Carlysle and his wife needing a room, and, contrary to spy fiction, the lovely Doctor Fletcher planning to spend the night with Mrs. Dumbrowski rather than Kearney. Kearney hoped the couch was comfortable.

"Kearney?"

It was Carlysle, a little blued Smith & Wesson Chiefs Special .38 in his right hand, held a little awkwardly. "Yes?"

"Was I good back there? I mean, at the mental hospital, in the derring-do department?"

"Excellent, Carlysle. I couldn't have asked for a

better man to partner with on it," Kearney said sincerely.

"I never trained for this sort of thing. That's why those guns of the opposition people you lent me emptied out so quickly. I haven't fired a pistol in almost a decade. Wondering if you'd take a look at my gun here, see if it's in order."

Kearney felt himself smile.

Carlysle handed it across, having emptied it first.

Kearney took the handgun, checked its unloaded condition for himself, then closed the cylinder. He held the gun so he could see it silhouetted against the light from the kitchen window. The spacing above and below the cylinder, in front and in back, was as it should be. He opened the cylinder, tilting the gun at an odd angle, spinning the cylinder on its base pin, the light between the spinning cylinder and lower portion of the frame even with no wobble.

Kearney closed the cylinder again. Holding the cylinder gently between the thumb and first two fingers of his left hand, he slowly thumb-cocked the gun. The cylinder was set before the hammer had finished its arc. "Ammunition fresh?"

"I change it every time I get a new box in the pouch. Last box was two months ago."

Kearney stepped deeper into the shadows, lit his Zippo, held the Zippo just away to the side of the open frame, and peered up the barrel. He could see the rifling clearly enough and there were no bore obstructions. "A good little gun. You should be right as rain," he told Carlysle, double-actioning the revolver, catching the hammer on the spur just before it fell, then easing it down gently. "You see," he said, by way of explanation, "I was trained for the field from the first. I never would have had the patience for what you do. I don't mean it as an insult, but a compliment instead. I just don't have it. I go bloody bonkers when all I'm doing is riding a desk. I'm not one of these fellows who's into danger and gets a thrill from it. I guess I'm just rather juvenile, perhaps. If it isn't something different, it gets to be a bore awfully fast." He laughed at himself. "Short attention span, I suppose."

Carlysle took the gun when Kearney offered it, methodically reloaded the five-round cylinder one cartridge at a time. "The Americans have the expression, I think. You're a jock. I'm not."

Kearney smiled. "Are all jocks strapping?"

Carlysle laughed. "Perhaps. I don't really care. I've always been happy as myself. Never much for the physical end of things, always the mental, always the detail man."

"I've always been enough with the mental side of it when the physical side of it was around the corner. As I said, perhaps I just never grew up."

"Odd thing, really," Carlysle said. "The thing at the mental hospital when we rescued the women. I enjoyed it, but I was frightened half out of my mind. You didn't look frightened at all."

Geoffrey Kearney told him, "Now, that's one thing that does come with experience in my end of the trade. You learn to hide the fear so very well they have to look deep into your eyes to see it, and when they pause to look that deeply, well, then you've got them."

Kearney clapped Carlysle on the shoulder.

"Melanie should have dinner ready I expect," Carlysle said.

Kearney told him, "There's where you've got it all over anything I could ever have. A girl like her. I mean that, Carlysle. I truly do."

He didn't. But Carlysle was a good man. . . .

Luther Steel almost tripped over Clark Pietrowski, then dropped to a crouch beside him in the small stand of pines about two hundred yards from the fence.

Runningdeer held his Uzi at high port, his Indian eyes peering into the night. Steel was struck that he held so many preconceptions about Runningdeer as an American Indian, yet hated preconceptions people had of him because he was black.

"The long-distance driver's inside there, and it looks like it's pretty tough to crack," Pietrowski commented, gesturing toward the rambling farmhouse beyond the fence. "I can't even risk a damn cigarette because they might see it," he added with an air of finality.

Steel studied the house. "Why's it so tough? I

mean, a lot of open ground and everything, but that fence is nothing."

"Ohh, yeah, but you didn't see the two guys with assault rifles like I did. And they were just on the front of the house and that was before dark. If Borsoi is alive, the motherfucker's got those street punks guarding the house. So, boss, what'll we do?"

"What you mean we, paleface?" Runningdeer laughed.

"Who are you calling 'paleface,' Bill?" Steel grinned. He hit the CB band walkie-talkie. "This is Bloodhound One. Come in, Bloodhound Three. Over."

Randy Blumenthal's voice came back. "This is Bloodhound Three, Bloodhound One. Two visible at the rear of the house, armed with M-16's or AR-15's. No way to tell. Tom's reconnoitering. Over."

"Get LeFleur back there, damn it. Nobody moves until I say so. Bloodhound One. Out."

"So, now that we know we're not supposed to recon the area, what are we supposed to do?" Pietrowski just looked at him.

Steel hissed, "I'm thinking, Clark. Take it easy. I'm thinking." He was thinking, but all the answers came out the same. Since it was impossible to call for backup, since they had no warrant, since they weren't certain at all of what they would find, the one answer he kept coming back to was to hit the house and, if they saw Borsoi, kill him.

But bad guys did that sort of thing. As a Federal

officer he was to arrest suspects, not try, convict, and execute them.

Clark Pietrowski must have seen it in his eyes, Steel realized. "You're up shit's creek, aren't you, boss? You can't go in there and be a cop. If you find this Borsoi creep, you can't arrest him. The case'd get tossed out, because you don't have a warrant. You probably don't even have probable cause. So what if he's there. There's never been an indictment against him. He doesn't officially exist, and even if he did, he's supposed to be dead."

"Shut up."

"The hell I will, boss. We go in there and we see what's inside and if what's inside looks like it needs flushin' down the toilet, we pull the chain and be done with it."

Runningdeer said, "He's right, Luther. Remember what those bastards did to Anna Comacho?"

The unit secretary, after having acid thrown in her face, was murdered in her hospital room.

"What's it gonna be, boss?" Pietrowski hissed.

Luther Steel took up the walkie-talkie from the ground beside his feet. "Bloodhound Three. Come in. Over."

"This is Bloodhound Three. Over."

"Tom back? Over."

There was a pause, then LeFleur's voice. "Right here, boss."

"You and Randy be ready. When you hear gunfire, come in fast and low, and for God's sake don't shoot us. This is Bloodhound One. Out."

146

Clark Pietrowski started laughing. Luther Steel checked the new SIG-Sauer P-226 from under his coat, reholstered it in the DeSantis rig. He looked at the police shotgun leaning against the tree stump. He'd always been taught never to stroke the pump and chamber a round until firing of the weapon was imminent. He picked up the Remington 870 and chunked the action. "I'm hot."

CHAPTER

25

It had been dark for some time. David Holden didn't know who the pickup truck that he found on the other side of the river belonged to, saint or sinner, but he stole it anyway. He abandoned it about two miles from what he judged the farthest boundary of Ortega de Vasquez's beyond-the-wall compound where Innocentio Hernandez and his men would be bunked.

Walking through the intermittent jungle in darkness unnerved him, but not so much as sleeping in it had that first night. And the pain in his abdomen was barely noticeable now, all but withdrawn. He moved as best he could, trying to maintain a constant level of alertness for any booby traps Hernandez's people might have laid, trying to convince himself he wasn't in some Southeast Asian country going up against communist guerrilla fighters. But the parallel was almost uncanny.

Every man he might meet was a potential enemy, out to kill him even if he weren't recognized. He was an armed stranger in their territory and that made him fair game for killing.

The weight of the four M-16's, the shotgun, the two handguns, the spare loose ammunition and loaded magazines made it necessary for him to stop twice. It was so much easier in the movies, the hero loaded down with enough weight to make a two-and-one-half ton truck's tires burst under it, but bounding along from one position of cover to the next. Maybe they were made of sterner stuff, David Holden told himself.

Holden was moving again, a faint corona of light barely visible when the tree cover parted. It would be Innocentio Hernandez's compound, which surrounded the walled house of Emiliano Ortega de Vasquez.

Somehow the light gave David Holden comfort. . . .

Luther Steel moved as quickly and silently as he could, the Remington 870 twelve-gauge in both fists, the collar of his suit coat turned up to cover his white shirt better, grateful for the color of his skin.

Beside him, Bill Runningdeer moved, but no more silently than he did, Steel told himself. The racial heritage of an American Indian was like any other racial heritage. Saying that all Indians were born with the ability to move silently was like saying that Clark Pietrowski, a Pole, had the congenital ability to make Polish sausage or that Steel's own children would slam dunk a basketball like the Harlem Globetrotters.

At last they reached the fence surrounding the farmhouse. It was an ordinary white painted board fence, flowerless rosebushes trellised over and through the slats. But the thorns would still be sharp, Steel reminded himself, almost reaching out to touch the fence. There was no evidence of electronic security, but Steel was certain that didn't mean that there wasn't any. It was just that he couldn't find it. Now was the time he could have used the rich and varied skills of Rocky Saddler, but at once Steel was glad the old black private detective wasn't here, was guarding his—Steel's—wife and children instead.

Steel signaled Runningdeer and Pietrowski, and they moved again, along the fence line and toward the driveway. Steel realized he had no choice but to dismiss electronic security from his mind. There might be alarms, cameras, lights, but there wouldn't be explosive charges rigged to go off. With the next house less than a mile away explosives were just too noisy.

He would take his chances.

They reached the driveway, still no evidence that they had caused some alarm to sound somewhere.

They huddled there on the boundary between the grass and the gravel driveway. "Anybody got any great suggestions? I'm not the world's greatest commando, as you guys may have noticed."

Pietrowski cleared his throat. "We go up on both sides of the driveway and get as close to the house as we can until the shooting starts, then keep going for the house. Best I can think of."

"That's a frontal assault," Bill Runningdeer interjected. "The Marines used those a lot. The casualties were high."

"Yes, but remember we have LeFleur and Blumenthal coming in from the rear once they hear gunfire," Pietrowski added, evidently enjoying himself.

"That makes it a kind of envelopment," Runningdeer told them.

Steel looked at him, "My son the tactician. You have hidden talents." Then he looked at Pietrowski. "We go up the middle, as you suggested. Fast. Once anybody starts shooting, we hit the house as quick as we can. God help us all."

Pietrowski looked up and down the drive and then crossed in a low run, reaching the other side of the fence. The gate was closed.

Steel was certain that opening the gate would trip an alarm, but that possibly flipping over it might not. Steel's right thumb pushed in against the next round up from the 870's tubular magazine. Slowly, his left thumb depressing the slide release latch forward of the trigger guard, Steel opened the action, just enough to start ejecting the chambered round of double-0 buckshot. He pulled it, verified the empty chamber tactilely, then closed the action, pointing the shotgun in a safe direction and snapping off the trigger. He fed the round removed from the chamber into the magazine. He'd learned enough about hunter safety as a boy that you didn't cross a fence with a loaded shotgun. He started going over the gate, the unnatural motion reminding him suddenly, painfully, of the grazing wound he'd sustained over his left rib cage when he and Rocky Saddler had held the upstairs corridor in the safe house in Wisconsin. Although only days ago, it seemed like years.

As Steel hit the ground, banks of floodlights positioned by the porch roof on either side of the house went on with an audible click, bathing the driveway and the grounds for a hundred yards on both sides of it in light bright enough to read by. Steel chunked the shotgun's pump.

"Stay down, boss!" Bill Runningdeer's voice. As Runningdeer opened fire with the Uzi, Steel told himself that even someone as good with a submachine gun as Runningdeer would be hard pressed for accuracy at this range, better than sixty yards. But lights started blowing out.

Steel started to run, toward the house as gunfire came at him from the artificial pitch blackness behind the lights. The 870's action just racked, Steel fired double-0 buck toward the lights. He kept running.

Steel looked over his shoulder. Clark Pietrowski

was running a zigzag pattern, pumping and firing his shotgun. More of the lights blew out. Bill Runningdeer was coming over the fence, caught one, and rolled into the grass. "Bill!"

Runningdeer sprayed out his submachine gun toward the lights, taking out four more of the bulbs, then shouted, "I'm all right!" Runningdeer was up, limping, but running.

Steel dived to cover behind a car. It was Humphrey Hodges's blue Volvo. The dirt and gravel on either side of the car was furrowing up under sustained gunfire. Steel drew the SIG-Sauer P-226 from the DeSantis shoulder rig he wore it in, stabbed the gun up over the Volvo's trunk lid, twisting the muzzle left and right and left, firing it out toward the front porch of the house.

He heard gunfire at a different pitch now, possibly coming from the rear of the house—LeFleur and Blumenthal.

Steel buttoned out the spent magazine in the SIG, pocketing it, and replaced it with one of the two twenties from the DeSantis rig's offside pouch.

"Clark?"

"I'm okay. So's Bill!"

Luther Steel was feeding double-0 buck from his pockets into the 870's magazine. "You guys ready?"

Clark Pietrowski's laughter came back from the darkness. "Like Ward Bond told the Duke that time, 'Hell, I was born ready!' "

"You'll know when!"

Steel was up, ripping open the Volvo's passenger door. He could figure out how to start it without any keys. But there wasn't any need. The keys were in the ignition. Steel stomped the clutch, turned the key, and floored the accelerator, holding the clutch down as he released the parking brake and found reverse.

He let up the clutch, the transmission smooth enough, the engine whining reassuringly. Gunfire hammered toward him.

He whipped the Volvo's steering wheel left, the rear end lining up. Gunfire tore into the windshield, shattering it as Steel tucked down, glass shards all over his jacket and his hands. He stomped the clutch, finding first and hitting the headlights. Steel flattened his foot to the floor over the accelerator. The Volvo punched forward into the darkness beyond the glare of the remaining floodlights. He hit something—steps—but the car, although it lurched and groaned and he was nearly thrown from the seat, started moving again, upward!

The Volvo slammed down hard. Gunfire came through the side window, blowing out the rearview mirror, punching into the upholstery, cutting a chip out of the steering wheel, but Steel remained still unwounded.

One of the Volvo's headlights was gone.

But in the glare of the other—he found the high-beam switch—he could see. A doorway. The Volvo punched through it as Steel wrenched open the Volvo's door handle, grabbing the 870 from the seat beside him, and rolled out from behind the wheel. Broken glass was everywhere, crunching under his knees and hands.

Movement. He rolled left, the flash of a submachine gun. Steel shouted, "Bill?"

"Not me!" More gunfire, suddenly more intense than before.

Steel fired, rolled, tromboning the shotgun's pump again, fired, rolled, worked the pump again. He jumped to his feet. The Volvo crashed into a wall and the single headlight went out.

Silence.

The tinkle of glass.

Then Steel squinted his eyes. Lights came on inside the house.

He dived left, toward the image of a piece of furniture almost burned into his eyes. He hit the floor hard. He was on his knees, feeding more rounds into the shotgun's tubular magazine.

"Hey, boss!"

Steel squinted past the couch he was kneeling behind.

He raised up slightly, the shotgun ready.

"I didn't mean to, damn it!"

It was Randy Blumenthal's voice. Then he heard Tom LeFleur saying, "You couldn't see a thing. Everybody was running like a fool out the back door and shooting at us."

Steel crossed from behind the couch, his eyes

adjusted to the light from the partially shot-out overhead fixture and the lamp in the far corner of the room. There were bullet holes in the wall all around the lamp and above it, the small table it stood on shot through several times as well. But the lamp was unscathed, except that somehow the shade was on crookedly, as if adjusted by a drunk.

Bill Runningdeer was limping toward the Volvo, leaned against it, his left trouser leg wet with blood.

"You making it?"

"I'm cool." Runningdeer nodded, his face locked in a grimace of pain, the Uzi tight in his right fist, his SIG-Sauer P-226 in his left.

Steel drew his own pistol from the waistband of his trousers.

Clark Pietrowski and Randy Blumenthal were standing in a doorway. No sign of Tom LeFleur. As Steel walked up to them, almost as if Pietrowski read his mind, the older man said, "Tom's okay. Just checking out the rest of this floor. There's a small upstairs. We'll get it in a second."

"Where's Hodges?"

"That's the problem, boss."

Luther Steel looked at Pietrowski, then to Randy Blumenthal's eyes. The young agent's face was flushed. There was a cut on his left cheek, presumably from glass. "I didn't know it was him, everybody shooting at us. I saw this guy and he was running and I drilled him."

Steel followed Blumenthal's gaze. In the corner

of the room—it was like a little parlor—there was a body, eyes open and staring up at the ceiling light.

"Shit," Luther Steel hissed.

It was Humphrey Hodges, dead with one neat bullet hole through the forehead, roughly between the eyes.

"Did you actually see him fall?"

Clark Pietrowski whispered, "You thinkin' what I think you're thinkin', boss? 'Cause I was thinkin' it first."

"Answer my question, Randy," Steel insisted, passing Blumenthal, going over to Humphrey Hodges's body.

"No, sir. But I saw movement. And then I fired and Hodges kind of fell against me. It all happened so fast."

Steel knelt beside the body. Clark Pietrowski dropped to his knees beside him. "You've seen a lot of homicides, haven't you, Clark?" Steel asked, his voice barely a whisper.

"You want a guess?"

Steel looked into the older man's eyes. "Yeah."

Pietrowski nodded, his hands already on the body. He called to Blumenthal. "Randy. Go find me a dead man who was farsighted and wore glasses—or if possible find a magnifying glass."

Steel stood up. He looked toward the Volvo. Bill Runningdeer leaned heavily against it. "You need medical attention right away?"

"I'm good for a few minutes. The bleeding's

pretty much stopped and I think the bullet went through."

"Can you keep an eye on the front door?"

"Gotchya, boss." Runningdeer—limping badly —moved off toward the front of the house. There was no door, no door frame, not much of anything except ragged sections of wall and empty windows.

"Tom?"

LeFleur's voice came from the side of the house. "Yo!"

"You take the upstairs. Everything that could conceivably be of any significance, bag it and bring it."

Blumenthal returned with a pair of glasses. Steel took them and aimed them toward the light. They magnified. "We'll let you know on this. Go check around downstairs. Like I told LeFleur."

"Yes, sir."

"Get a tissue or some toilet paper, Luther."

Steel nodded to Pietrowski, rubbing his side as he found the bathroom, got some toilet paper, and brought it back.

He gave it to Pietrowski. "You might wanna look away. Makes some people puke. Some tough people," Pietrowski noted.

Steel didn't look away, but a split second later wished that he had. Pietrowski daubed a single sheet of toilet paper on the open eyeball of Humphrey Hodges.

He bent over Hodges, studying the eyes with

the glasses, like some sort of Sherlock Holmes with a magnifying glass.

"He's been dead longer than he would have been if Randy'd iced him. You were right. For that matter, boss, so was I." And he looked up and smiled. "The eyeballs are almost dry. It isn't that hot in the house here, so there should have been more moisture if he'd died within the last six or seven minutes. Randy didn't do it. One of the FLNA did it."

"Police'll be coming," Steel said, amazed at his words as they came from his lips. "We'd better get out of here, fast."

"Yeah, they catch us with this dead solid citizen and the wrecked house, Makowski'll have all he needs."

Steel's and Pietrowski's eyes met. "What that implies is absurd," Steel murmured.

"You just keep saying that, Luther. All the way to jail." Pietrowski stood up, shouted, "Randy. Tom. Clean up any prints you might have left. Be quick about it." Then he started walking toward the Volvo.

"What the hell are you doing?"

"I'm wiping your fingerprints off the damn car, Luther. Eventually they'll get some latents off cartridge cases. We can't do anything about that, but we don't have to give it to them. They set us up, damn it."

Luther Steel felt like vomiting. Instead he took out his handkerchief and headed for the bathroom. He'd touched the doorknob.

CHAPTER

26

Just after taking one last step and an instant before the Hernandez man turned around, David Holden punched the Defender knife into the carotid artery at the right side of the man's neck. The man's eyes went wide with death as Holden averted his face so he wouldn't get blood in his own eyes or mouth, then eased the body down into the broad-leafed, bright green foliage, almost soundlessly.

Quickly Holden wiped the blade of the knife clean on the man's trouser leg, then sliced through web gear with it, denuding the man of weapons and equipment. Holden stole back into the trees.

The man had been armed with an Uzi. Holden took this, checking first that it seemed wholly functional, then donning the magazine bag, knotting the strap he'd sliced through to a convenient height.

The pistol and knife were only surpassed in their ordinariness by their poor condition. He disarmed the pistol, then hid the weapons in the jungle.

He started moving again.

Another sentry, just barely detectable, stood about two hundred yards off and close to the gate in the perimeter fence surrounding the Hernandez compound which, in turn, surrounded the Ortega de Vasquez estate. Holden would never have seen the man had he not been backlit by the compound security lights.

Holden moved toward the man, cautious lest he be detected. Camouflage clothing would have helped earlier in the day, but in its absence Holden could not use what native material was available, the terrain and its foliage changing so quickly that what might have worked in one spot would merely have drawn attention to his presence a hundred or two hundred yards away. So he relied on darkness, his face and hands blackened with charcoal, but perspiration rapidly diminishing its effectiveness.

He did the best he could, moving on the second man. . . .

Rose Shepherd folded the black bandana into a triangle, tossing her hair back, binding the bandana over it, around it, knotting it at the nape of her neck. The second bandana she folded into a triangle as well, knotting this one bandit fashion over the lower portion of her face, between the two scarves only her eyes and a small portion of her forehead visible as she looked at herself in the small metal mirror hung inside the van.

She stood up, into a crouch, pulling on the black cloth fingerless gloves.

The Glock pistol, the lightweight Glock fighting knife, the Uzi submachine gun, were all as they should be.

Tom Ashbrooke already crouched by the rear doors, black garbed and armed identically to her.

Rose Shepherd moved toward the door. "Ready. And thanks, however this turns out, Tom." She pulled down the bandana, which covered her face, then pulled down his and kissed him quickly on the mouth. She slid the door open, then stepped out into the night.

The Israeli commando personnel waited.

"Let's go," Rose Shepherd hissed through the bandana as, once again, she covered her face.

CHAPTER
27

The fence was ten feet high, topped by electrified barbed wire, reminiscent of concentration or POW camps, beyond the outer fence an inner fence made of barbed wire. The space between, Holden realized, must be laid with mines. It would have been possible to scale the fence and cross over the electrified barbed wire, but not with all of the equipment he carried. And the equipment could not be tossed over the fence without possible risk of activating one of the land mines.

He sat in a high tree, grateful for the lack of daylight. It was probably filled with ants and in darkness he couldn't see them. He contemplated his next move carefully, because it would be pivotal not only to his success in eradicating Hernandez and Ortega de Vasquez, but to any chance of escape with his life.

An instructor he'd had in his SEAL Team days,

ostensibly a civilian, an older man who could have been doing the "commando number," as the fellow had called it, during World War Two, had told Holden that the key to success in an operation was the insight one brought to it. If the operation were conceived of as hopelessly complicated, the means for carrying it out would be even more hopelessly complicated. Simplicity, based on insight, was the key to success. The more to do, the more to go wrong.

Digging under the fence, dragging the equipment through beneath it, all the while hoping not to be spotted or activate an alarm, then painstakingly navigating the mine field only to reach the other fence, crossing over or under it, then sneaking through the Hernandez compound to reach the estate grounds was the obvious answer.

Perhaps not the best.

If he could make Hernandez's personnel think that they were being attacked in force, his interests might best be served. There was the risk of losing Hernandez himself that way, but it would be less of a risk than getting killed without reaching either man he sought.

David Holden studied the tree around him.

David Holden cupped his hands around the liberated cigarette lighter and lit his last cigarette. Hidden in the trees as he was, chances were minimal of being noticed. And it might be the last thing he would ever do. . . .

* * *

They were a quarter mile off the road, in a rocky area, bright moonlight bathing the mountain top in glaring brightness. She shifted the weight of the musette bag in which she carried the .44 Magnum Desert Eagle and the spare magazines for it. She would give the contents of the bag to David Holden, or die trying.

They kept their faces masked because the support personnel, six of them, all Israeli university students from a neighboring country, were safer not knowing any faces. The six were involved in the operation as support personnel only and had met none of the team and were recruited by an Israeli agent specifically for this purpose. Rose Shepherd was almost as uncomfortable, her face and hair swathed in black bandanas, as she was when, with the Patriots, she would occasionally use a hood to cover her face. Almost as uncomfortable, but not quite.

The Israeli commando leader spoke in rapid-fire Hebrew, the female member of the team doing a running rough translation for Rose and Tom Ashbrooke.

"He is telling the young man named Moishe that the success or failure of the entire operation hinges on the wind currents. If the currents are not right, we cannot go tonight."

"The hell with that," Rose Shepherd told her. "We go tonight."

The woman said nothing, but Rose could watch

the portion of the bandana over the woman's mouth suck inward, push outward as she breathed. There was silence among the six men and the Israeli leader for a moment. And Rose Shepherd studied the hang gliders there on the mountaintop. There were anemometers of some sort spinning, but erratically. At least she thought the thing's wind speed and current were judged with were called anemometers. David would know.

She inhaled suddenly, tasting the fabric of the black bandana against her lips, almost saying his name aloud.

The woman took up her translation duties again. "The tall man who is speaking now says that he has used gliders like these that we have brought several times with winds such as these and the winds are unpredictable. But he would try it." And the bandana sucked in deeply over her lips as she went to speak, but didn't.

"What?" Tom Ashbrooke asked her.

The Israeli woman said, "He told the captain that the worst which could happen is we would be killed. But if we wait a few hours, the winds might change."

Rose Shepherd stared at the anemometer thing. . . .

David Holden moved as quickly as he could, securing ropes of vine, making their tails obvious so he could locate them quickly in the moonlight. The task consumed more time than he'd thought

166

it would, building for himself a sort of treetop expressway, testing each vine with his weight, orienting himself on some landmark or another so he would be able to pick his next position quickly, most probably under fire.

"Should have watched more Tarzan movies," Holden hissed under his breath.

At last the work was finished, the face of his Rolex reading nearly two A.M. So much for catching Hernandez and Ortega de Vasquez at dinner together.

He returned to the original tree, the slow way, on the ground. He checked the cache of weapons he had made there. The Uzi, two of the M-16's, an assortment of spare magazines and loose ammunition were where he had left them.

Holden checked his own body equipment one last time. Two M-16's, the two Beretta pistols, plenty of spare magazines for the firearms and the Defender knife.

Holden started up into the tree. . . .

Rose Shepherd studied the face of the Timex Ironman watch, the digital readout showing just after two A.M. She was tired of standing around or sitting around, tired of concealing her face, tired of watching the erratic revolutions of the anemometer thing.

But as she looked at it once again, she noticed that it turned regularly now, evenly. She kept watching it, as if somehow taking her eyes from it would alter its regularity, sabotage their attempts to rescue David.

The Israeli woman used a hand-held radio transmitter, speaking in Hebrew.

She put the transmitter down. "The front we have been waiting for. Our source in the weather service says it is passing through. It was stalled, but is passing through. It should become cool very quickly, but the wind should hold."

She went toward the leader, who was already conferring with the one of the six young Israelis identified as Moishe.

Tom Ashbrooke pulled off his glove and held Rose Shepherd's hand. . . .

David Holden set the sights of the M-16, on safe still, where he would have planted a cluster of land mines. He held the position for as long as it would have taken to fire a real burst, then slung the rifle quickly, reached out, grabbed the vine rope, and moved almost as far along the limb as he would need to to jump clear.

In theory it worked like a charm. . . .

The Israeli captain explained in English as he and the woman and two of the men set out their gliders, the six Israeli university students assisting them. "The wingspan of Rachel's glider is only 22.1 feet, because she weighs 110 pounds and with all of her equipment the combined weight won't exceed 155 pounds. That gives her a little over 192 square feet of wing area to support her body. With too little wing area she might not get off the ground, certainly wouldn't be able to do it easily, and soaring would be more difficult. With a larger kite, like mine for example—I weigh 182 pounds and carry more equipment, so my wingspan is 25.8 feet and my sail area is almost 268 square feet —she'd have substantial control difficulties."

He pointed the nose area of the huge kitelike affair into the wind. "Using ridge lift, thermals, like that, we can get astonishingly high, but we're not looking for any more height than we'll need this time around. We intend to soar over the compound, dropping gas grenades out of the night sky, reaching the grassy area inside the walls of the estate where Ortega de Vasquez actually lives. Once the first grenade is dropped, you and the rest of the team enter as we discussed."

There were wires, apparently for front and back and both sides, some of the wires shorter. A bar that looked like something stolen off an exotic bicycle was unpacked. He took a tool from a small kit and set to checking a bolt.

Rachel looked up from her wings, saying, "I hope you find him. We'll all be praying for you."

Rose Shepherd said thanks, then saw that Tom Ashbrooke was signaling her back toward the trucks. "Thanks," she repeated, and walked after Tom Ashbrooke, feeling the weight of the Desert Eagle more heavily on her shoulders . . .

* * *

David Holden settled himself into a comfortable, solid kneeling position in the notch of the tree limb.

He set the M-16's selector to full auto.

He aimed at the area he had previously targeted, about four feet inside the outer fence, an area where the first step in a man's cautious stride after passing over the fence would put his foot on a land mine.

David Holden opened fire, zigzagging the muzzle of the 5.56mm assault rifle right and left and right and up and down, a good ten rounds fired as the explosions started, puffs of gray-white smoke and dust flying upward in a ragged wall.

The selector moved to safe under his thumb and he slung the rifle behind him, reaching for the vine rope, stepping up and forward simultaneously.

No fire from the compound yet. He held to the rope and pushed off, sailing out between the tree from which he'd fired and the tree to which the vine rope was attached, for all the world wanting to imitate Johnny Weissmuller's famous yell.

Holden refrained.

He reached the tree limb he wanted to reach within seconds, congratulating himself, climbed into the notch, shifting the M-16 forward, flicking off the safety to full auto, his target already selected, lined up on line of sight with a bit of cloth tied to a leaf stem, the cloth torn from the handkerchief he'd been given along with the clothes.

Holden opened fire, hitting the other side of the gate now. He could count at least five mines exploding. His task was easier now because he had the pattern set in his mind by which they'd been placed, like interlocking points of a compass.

About ten rounds again. Safety on. Rifle slung. He reached for the next vine rope, pushed away from the limb and into free air as gunfire tore into the tree where he'd just been.

Holden miscalculated, barely able to catch the limb, partially body-slamming into the trunk, the wind knocked out of him. But he didn't lose his handhold. "Hell of a Jungle Jim I'd make," Holden snarled at himself. He swung up into the limb, moved along its length.

Into the notch. Confirm the target designator cloth strip. Set to full auto.

Holden opened fire, snapping off three rounds to the far side of the gate, setting off two more mines, cleaning the magazine of the remaining six or seven rounds into the near side, activating three more mines.

Holden buttoned the magazine release, stuffed the magazine into the ditty bag, fed a fresh one, chambered the top round, set the safety, reached for the vine rope and sprang out, gunfire tearing into the trunk of the tree, shredding leaves on the branches all around him.

He reached the next limb, slickly, climbing into the notch.

Target designator. He opened fire, exploding two more land mines, and scoring a half-dozen shots into the gasoline storage tank near the garage. Nothing happened for a moment, then the tank exploded, the night air suddenly brighter than it had been in the moonlight as the crackle of flames, yellow light, and a black fireball dispersed into the night sky.

A two-man team was setting up a machine gun, aiming it toward the trees. Holden fired a three-round burst, then another, getting both men.

Safe the rifle. Grab the vine rope. Jump.

Gunfire was everywhere around him now, leaves thwacking into his face, chunks of bark spraying around him as he reached the next limb, climbed into the notch.

Holden fired out the magazine, killing three more of the Hernandez men, shooting out the windshield of a pickup truck.

Change magazines. Jump.

Holden swung to the ground.

He shoved aside the leaves and foliage covering his other weapons, grabbed up the weapons on slings, slung them to his body. The shotgun was into his fists.

David Holden ran, keeping as low as he could, all the gunfire coming from the Hernandez compound aimed into the upper level of trees, not ground level.

There was a gaping hole in the outside fence, the ground beyond it cratered from the exploding mines. Holden ran for the gap, through it, along the center between the two fences, sticking to the cratered areas. He reached another gap, in the interior fence.

Holden went through.

A man to his left. Holden fired the shotgun, pumped it, fired again.

Pump the shotgun.

Run.

Two men.

A third. Holden grabbed at the Uzi with his left hand, worked the safety off, and stabbed it toward the three, firing, spraying out the entire magazine, bringing the three men down. He let the Uzi fall to his side on its sling.

He was running again.

He was in the compound street with the bunkhouses with their air-conditioning units and so many lights on. Lights were on in the house where Hernandez slept.

Holden ran toward it.

Three men came around from the side of Hernandez's house.

Holden fired the shotgun, pumped, fired, pumped, fired, pumped. He downed the three men. Holden threw the shotgun away, grabbing up an M-16 in each hand, running for Hernandez's house.

A man raced through the doorway, and for a

173

moment Holden thought it might be Innocentio Hernandez, the drug smuggler, the man who enjoyed killing. But there was no bearlike stature here, this just an ordinary man.

With a short burst from both M-16's simultaneously, this ordinary man was dead.

Holden sprayed both weapons across the front of the house, let them fall to his sides on their slings, taking up the other two.

He had the safeties off, ran up the steps, into the house through the wide open doorway.

There was no one inside.

Holden swapped magazines in the spent M-16's and the Uzi.

As he stepped back onto the porch, he saw a man flying through the air and there was a small explosion and a cloud of gas sprang up from the ground.

"What the—"

Holden ran, toward the wall separating the Hernandez compound from the Ortega de Vasquez estate proper.

A man was driving an open-top Jeep from the Ortega de Vasquez house. Holden ran for him. Another flying man, another gas grenade. Holden held his breath as the cloud neared him.

The man in the Jeep swerved toward him. David Holden fired, fired again and again. The windshield shattered out, the man slumped over the steering wheel.

Still holding his breath, Holden dodged right,

ran, jumped, and, barking his shins on the Jeep's coachwork, grabbed the wheel, twisting it out of the dead man's grasp. Then he jumped in beside him, rolling the body out the other side.

Holden stomped the brake, found reverse, and stepped on the gas.

The gas cloud was nearly surrounding him. Holden cut the wheel right, changing into a forward speed—he didn't know which one—and stomped the gas pedal. Not much happened. Holden downshifted, then again, stomping the gas, and the Jeep lurched ahead. Holden averted his eyes as shards of glass fell from the shot-out windshield.

He was out of the gas cloud, coughing as he let the stale air out of his lungs and gulped fresh.

The wall of the Ortega de Vasquez estate was in front of him.

Holden aimed the Jeep for it. . . .

Rose Shepherd crouched beside the door of the van, one of the Israelis throwing it open. There was already a battle going on here. But with whom?

She stabbed the Uzi through the open doorway and fired, anything that moved here (unless it was David or one of the penetration team) a fair target. A man went down, then another and another.

Thomas Ashbrooke knelt in the opposite side of the doorway, pulling the pin on a canister-shaped gas grenade, flinging it out the door.

Rose Shepherd fired out the stick in the Uzi and tucked back, loading a fresh magazine up the well, then punching the submachine gun through the opening, firing again.

Overhead, she could see the last of the four Israelis. Somehow, she knew it was Rachel, the body more graceful despite the bulky gear.

A gas grenade hit the ground and detonated.

Rose Shepherd would clearly have preferred the black bandana she'd worn to hide her identity from the Israeli students to the sweltering heat of the gas mask she wore now. But the gas was some type of knockout gas, one of many variants of sodium-based types, some of which she'd seen in action years ago as a demonstration when a quantity of gas had been stolen from a military base near Metro and the police had been brought in to help locate the thieves.

Headache city, she thought.

She kept firing. . . .

David Holden held the Uzi in his left fist, firing it as he drove, cutting down Hernandez's men as he accelerated toward the hedgerow and the wall surrounding the Ortega de Vasquez house.

There were men coming down from the sky, in hang gliders, coasting over the grass beyond the wall, hurtling gas grenades as they descended.

One flew overhead.

Who were they?

Holden kept driving. . . .

* * *

Rose Shepherd suddenly had an idea.

She spoke into the microphone built into the gas mask. "Rescue Leader, this is Rescue Eleven. Come in, Rescue Leader."

The Israeli commando captain, the other two men with him, and the woman all had combination crash helmet/gas masks with built-in radio send/receive units. But were they in range. "This is Rescue Leader, Rescue Eleven. Reading you loud and clear. What is wrong? Over."

"The gun battle down here, Rescue Leader. What if David is part of it?"

"The gas will not kill. I say again, the gas will not kill, Rescue Eleven."

"Be on the lookout for him, Rescue Leader. Please. Out."

It was just a feeling, but it was so strong she was starting to feel sick in the pit of her stomach.

She was up, running forward in the van to the driver. "Get across this compound, quick, man! Just do it!"

"We are supposed to hold the outer compound, Detective Shepherd," the Israeli told her.

Rose Shepherd stabbed the Uzi toward his face. "I can drive this damn van, too, buddy boy. What's it gonna be?"

"You cannot be—"

Rose Shepherd just stared at him, the muzzle of the submachine gun inches from his face. She wouldn't have shot him, just cold-cocked him and grabbed the wheel, but he didn't know that.

"Yes." he nodded, the voice sounding odd echoing, audible through the gas mask and through the radio within it. He cut the wheel left and Rose Shepherd held on. . . .

David Holden shot a man holding an M-16 with a full-auto burst in the face, then cut the Jeep's steering wheel hard right and across the lawn, trying to avoid another of the gas clouds.

There were four men on the ground now, disconnecting themselves from the hang gliders on which they'd come, the helmets they wore completely covering the face, gas masks built in, he supposed.

There was a gas cloud on either side of him, boxing him in.

David Holden gambled, cutting the wheel left, toward the nearest of the four hang-glider pilots, the last to land.

He started shouting. "I'm on your side! Do you hear me? The gas! Do you have a mask?"

The clouds were closing around him. . . .

They were cutting through the compound now, the gas already dissipating, men's bodies strewn everywhere, many of them visibly the victims of gunshot wounds. David? Rose Shepherd wondered.

Past a house—the windows shot out, a dead man on the porch.

Skid marks on the road surface.

The hedgerows and the wall surrounding the Ortega de Vasquez house lay ahead.

"You wouldn't have shot me, miss," the man from behind the wheel said suddenly.

Rose Shepherd looked at him. He looked like some outer-space bad guy with the gas mask in place. But his eyes, visible through the mask, smiled. "You are in love with this man!"

"No shit, Sherlock"—and Rose Shepherd laughed.

Ahead of them gas clouds were everywhere.

But where was David?

She felt the van speeding up. . . .

David Holden slowed the Jeep. The man from the fourth hang glider had to be a woman, and she held an Uzi aimed right at his chest.

He gambled again. "What are you doing here?"

She lowered the Uzi. Her voice was terribly muffled by the mask. "So. This is why Detective Shepherd is so obsessed. You are good looking." And then she reached into a khaki bag at her side and drew a gas mask from it, tossing it to him. "Rescue Leader and all personnel. We have Holden. He's all right." David Holden didn't understand. But he pulled on the mask. . . .

* * *

Rose Shepherd couldn't see. Suddenly her eyes were streaming tears and the eyepieces in her mask were covered with them and she couldn't stop crying.

CHAPTER

28

They would risk removing their gas masks, the Israeli commandos from the van and the three men and the woman who had landed in the yard in defensive positions near the truck.

And Tom Ashbrooke was there.

The voice was distorted, because of the mask, when Tom said, "I'm glad you're alive, son," to David.

David Holden pulled off his mask.

Rose Shepherd pulled off hers.

They crouched inside the van.

He touched her face.

Tears were in her eyes.

David Holden folded her into his arms and kissed her. . . .

Rose Shepherd was staring at him. She jumped down from the van.

David Holden, his voice sounding odd to him through the mask, said to her, "Why are you looking at me like that?"

"You wouldn't understand. Even though you're the nicest guy I ever met and if any guy would understand, you would, but you wouldn't. We still got business here?"

"Emiliano Ortega de Vasquez and Innocentio Hernandez. They killed a woman named Maria— Hernandez actually did the shooting—and she helped me to get out of here. He just murdered her."

"Then let's do it, David, and get out of here."

Crouching in the door of the van, David Holden saw his father-in-law and embraced the man. . . .

The house was surrounded, four of the Israelis at the front and four at the back.

David Holden, Rose Shepherd, Tom Ashbrooke, the Israeli captain and the female commando, Rachel, closed on the front door of the Ortega de Vasquez mansion.

The Israeli woman, the rest of them covering her, applied a thin strip of plastique to the juncture of the two doors, running a detonator wire from the plastique back to cover.

Holden watched through the eyepieces of his gas mask.

Rachel stripped away the ends of the two wires emanating from the main and touched one to a small storage battery, wrapping it on the terminal.

She looked at the rest of them.

The commando captain nodded.

She touched the second wire to the second terminal.

The doors seemed to buckle inward in a puff of smoke.

Holden was up and running with Rosie Shepherd beside him. And that was a good feeling. He hadn't told her he loved her, that he missed her. But he thought she knew it.

They were through the blown-out doorway, Holden and Rosie to the right, the Israeli captain and Rachel crisscrossing to the left, and Tom Ashbrooke beside the doors, an Uzi in each hand.

Holden stopped in the main hall.

He turned toward the library.

The doors were ajar.

"Watch out, David," Rosie's voice whispered through the headset in the gas mask.

David Holden walked slowly toward the library.

Sitting at the desk, he could see Emiliano Ortega de Vasquez.

Standing beside Ortega de Vasquez was Innocentio Hernandez, seeming bigger than Holden remembered him. Hernandez was smiling.

Ortega de Vasquez stood up slowly from behind the desk, his nattily tailored suit perfect, his hair perfect. Everything about him was as perfect and neat as Innocentio Hernandez was imperfect, animallike.

"I will make you what you Americans like to call a deal, Professor Holden."

David Holden, Rosie, Tom Ashbrooke, and the two Israelis behind him stood in the library doorway.

Ortega de Vasquez continued speaking. "What I know is very valuable to you and your so-called Patriots. In return for my life and, when I have told you what you wish, my freedom, I will willingly tell you everything. The names, inside the Soviet Union, of the men who wish to see warfare because it brings them money, the names of the public officials within the United States who work with the Front for the Liberation of North America. All of the details of the drug shipments, the explosives, everything. In exchange for my life—and the life of Hernandez, of course."

David Holden tore off his gas mask, the Uzi still in his right hand. "Would it sour the deal if Señor Hernandez here weren't a part of it?"

Hernandez's smile faded. He looked at Ortega de Vasquez.

Ortega de Vasquez moved away from him.

Ortega de Vasquez smiled and said, "No, Professor Holden."

David Holden turned to look at Hernandez. Innocentio Hernandez said, laughing, but the laughter tinged with the hollow sound of bravado, not amusement, "You are an American, huh! Americans do not murder people, huh! I spit on you, because you will not kill me! I have rights and you know that I do! Stupid American!"

"Maria," David Holden whispered, stretching out his right hand and touching the first finger of his right hand to the Uzi's trigger. The submachine gun bucked in his hand and Innocentio Hernandez's face and neck and chest seemed to melt away.

Holden turned his back. Rosie had her gas mask off. He folded her into his arms, closing his eyes.